IN THE TALE

A Collection of Short Stories

by

THOMAS JACKSON

Published by

Thomas Jackson
Holly Cottage
Lodsworth
West Sussex GU28 9BZ

Published 2017

Author's Note These short stories are works of fiction. The names, characters and incidents portrayed in them are mainly the work of the author's imagination.

Set in Palatino Linotype and printed in Great Britain by Spiffing Covers

ABOUT THE AUTHOR

Thomas Jackson worked in advertising for over 40 years, finding time to write his first novel *A Corsican Affair* which is being reprinted in April 2018. Rosamunde Pilcher, author of *The Shell Seekers,* clearly enjoyed it, commenting wryly. "This is a rip-roaring adventure, full of colour, excitement and intrigue".

A Sting in the Tale is his second book, and is a collection of short stories.

The author lives in Lodsworth, West Sussex, and also in Villecroze in Provence, with his wife Annie and their liver and white Springer Spaniel - Charlie

Thomas's interests include golf, photography, reading, writing, 60's music and generally enjoying life.

ACKNOWLEDGEMENTS

Annie, my family and all my friends who have helped me live through this long journey

Fleur O'Kelly for safeguarding my original manuscript

Special thanks to Caroline Morris for editing/proof reading and also her undying patience and belief

Kate Prickett who has been an inspiration

James Willis and all the team at Spiffing Covers for their wonderful creativity and patience

Emily and Rachel at Blackdown Design, for their clever use of Adobe InDesign

And, you of course, for buying this book!

CONTENTS

TWO PARROTS

The Woodwards were to all intents and purposes a happy, but rather ordinary family. They lived on the outskirts of Bristol, in a small semi-detached house, along with many other small, nondescript, semi-detached houses. Pebble dash was the order of the day, and Mrs Woodward, Shirley, kept her house neat and tidy always giving a warm welcome to visitors, with the inevitable, "I'm sure you'd love a cup of tea dear", or a similar greeting.

When she had first married Keith she'd been a shy young thing of eighteen, but as the years wore on she had gained in confidence, and was now considered a pillar of the community, particularly the church. Anything that needed doing for the church Shirley would do, right down to scrubbing the altar's steps. This religious zeal was not shared by her husband.

'I just can't see what you get out of going to church every Sunday and sometimes during the week,' said Keith over breakfast one Sunday morning. 'I'm sure the children don't thank you for insisting they go with you. It's not as if we're Roman Catholics.'

Their children, Tracy and Angela, both in their teens, kept well out of this on-going discussion. They quite liked going to Matins with their Mum, which wasn't until late on Sunday mornings, thus giving them a good lie-in, following Saturday night's inevitable partying.

Tracy was the prettier of the two, with long blonde hair and piercing blue eyes. Angela was rounder but rather jollier, with mousy hair and an engaging smile. They went to the local grammar school, where Tracy was finishing her A levels and Angela was doing her GCSEs.

'I don't know why you always have the same conversation with Mum. It's not as though she interferes with your life,' Tracy said to her father, one evening at supper. 'At least she has a life. The church is very important to her and she does a lot of honest, charitable work, which is more than can be said about you.' Whereupon she sat back in her chair and eye-balled her father.

'Now, now Tracy. You know you shouldn't talk to your father like that,' her mother interjected. 'Each to their own is my maxim in life.'

'It's just, Mum, that Dad's often not around. If it's not his work then it's his golf. At least the three of us see each other occasionally. It's Thursday today and this is the first time this week Dad's been home for supper.'

'May I have a word?' their Dad said, plainly not happy about the criticism being levelled at him. 'You must remember I work long hours to provide a decent home for you lot. Do you think I actually enjoy having to sometimes work a twelve hour day? Frankly I'm lucky to have a job at all. People at the factory are being laid off daily, and I consider myself fortunate that I've found my niche in the business, and kept my head down. So just remember how much I contribute to the family's coffers, and we'll have no more of your snide comments Tracy. If you don't like it you can forget about going to university. Just get yourself a job and move out.'

'Don't worry Dad. I'll go to university, even if I have to pay my own way. I'm not afraid of working.' So saying she thanked her mother for supper, and left the kitchen in one of her moods.

'Now look what you've done Keith.'

'Mum, don't worry about it. Tracy's being Tracy. We're all as used to her outbursts as we are of not seeing a lot of Dad. Anyway Dad I'm proud of you, and I know Tracy is really. By the way, why are you home so early today?'

'Can't you guess?' said her mother. 'He's probably off to the driving range or playing a few holes before sunset. Am I right darling?'

'Yes, yes,' Keith said resignedly, 'I hope you don't mind dear.'

'Mind. Why should I?' she replied. 'It's your life and as long as we muddle along happily I have no problem at all. It's only Tracy that has a problem and I think she's getting a bit uptight about her A levels. After all they're only a few weeks away now.'

'What about my GCSEs then? I think I'm going to start being moody,' Angela said laughing at the very thought.

'Well I'm off to a church council meeting,' Shirley said loading the dishwasher. 'What time will you be back Keith, are you meeting up with Dave?'

'Yes. I'll just give him a call. We'll probably have a couple of pints after the game so see you about tennish.'

'Okay. Have fun. Heavens, is that the time? I must fly. See you later then.'

'Bye, Mum. Bye, Dad. Don't you worry about me. You both go out and enjoy yourself, and I'll go and do a spot of geography revision.'

The church was only a few minutes walk for Shirley, so Keith took their car, and drove quickly to the golf course, as he was already running late. Green Lands Golf Club was a good challenging course and membership was Keith's only real luxury in life. In return he paid for Shirley's annual "girlie" week in Majorca. That way there was no animosity, although clearly Keith benefitted more in the long run as he played a lot of golf.

'Hurry up Keith,' Dave shouted, as Keith was parking his car, 'we're due on the first tee in 10 minutes."

It was a gorgeous evening and, as Keith's drive flew at least 270 yards down the middle of the fairway, he felt on top of the world. He was looking forward to the golf, and his drink in the bar afterwards, with his best mate Dave.

Dave had been his best man and had two boys close in age to Keith's children. The two families had been going on their summer holidays together since their children were born. It had always worked well, although the two eldest were beginning to want to do their own thing. But as both the fathers pointed out to their respective children, "there's nothing cheaper than free". There were no secrets between Keith and Dave. When Dave had been having an affair with a secretary from work, Keith was happy to vouch for his friend's whereabouts, usually "on the golf course" was the fabricated story. Fortunately it had been a summer affair, so Keith's job was made easier, and in the end the whole thing had evaporated after a couple of steamy months. This complicity had the effect of bonding the two men more closely together. So Dave was very excited when, on the ninth and final green, Keith had said.

'I've got something very juicy to tell you. Let's get to the bar and I'll order us a couple of pints. You won't believe what I've been up to recently!'

Meanwhile back at the church meeting, Shirley was not a happy woman when she heard the vicar's news. The vicar, Reverend Josh Nicholls, who had been with the local church for over seven years, had just received a posting to the English church in Florence. He was a very keen art lover, and always took his holidays in Tuscany. His children had grown up and left the Vicarage and both he and his wife felt they could not pass up such a wonderful opportunity. But it was doubly sad for Shirley. She and Jean, the vicar's wife, were good friends and Josh's pastoral care had converted her from being a very occasional churchgoer, to being a regular one.

After the meeting Josh came up to Shirley and, putting a sympathetic arm around her shoulder, said,

'Of all the parishioners, Jean and I will certainly miss you the most. I love my flock but you've become such a good and loyal friend I just don't know how I would have run the parish without you.'

With tears welling up in her eyes, and hugging Josh she said.

'You and the church have changed my life, there's no doubt about that. I can't tell you my immediate thoughts, but my Christian ones are that you deserve this break, and I'm sure you'll be very happy. For the moment let's enjoy your ministering for these last few months and welcome your replacement with open arms.'

'I knew I could count on that sort of reaction from you,' and he kissed her gently on both cheeks.

His wife then came up to him and said,

'Now you put her down! What you're going to be like

in Florence, with all the smart ex-pats and Signoras, let alone the Signorinas, I shudder to think. Anyway Shirley come back and have a glass of wine at the Vicarage, there's something I want to ask you.'

The three of them walked arm in arm through the churchyard to the Vicarage. Once inside Jean called out:

'Red or white tonight Shirley?'

'Red please. Thanks.'

They sat in the cosy sitting room and Shirley remarked how quiet Freddie, the parrot, was.

'That's what I wanted to talk to you about. As you know Freddie's really very old, and we think the journey to Florence and the heat will probably be too much for him. I know how much you love him and I was wondering whether you'd look after him for us.'

'Do you mean for good?'

'Yes. Yes. Although whenever we come back we'd obviously want to see you, and that way we get to see Freddie as well. What do you think?'

'I think it's a wonderful idea. When you're gone there'll still be a small member of the Nicholls' family in my home. Thank you so much for asking me to be a surrogate mother. I think it's a grand idea. I know the children will be chuffed,' Shirley said excitedly.

'Good. Well that's settled then. It's weird actually because he's been very quiet since we heard about Florence, haven't you Freddie?'

Indeed the parrot didn't look too happy, but Shirley assured them that he'd perk up in their house.

Meanwhile, at the golf club Dave was hanging on Keith's every word.

'You remember I told you my boss wanted to take me out

one evening to discuss business,' Keith said.

'Yes I do. You were a bit worried weren't you? So what happened?' Dave asked.

'Well, it's strange because George acted totally out of character. It was as though he was a sort of Jekyll and Hyde character. At the office he's authoritarian, and doesn't suffer fools gladly at all. However, when he came round by taxi to pick me up, he looked really cool in smart chinos, a T-shirt and a very well-cut leather jacket. And, would you believe, cowboy boots? Fortunately he'd said dress casually. Anyway our first port of call was that trendy "Legends" bar near the canal. It was heaving, and there was crumpet to die for. George said to me, "You haven't seen anything yet." So I knew we were in for quite an evening. From there we went to Jo's Brasserie for dinner, and he told me about his boring marriage, and how his teenage children didn't understand him, and how he just wanted someone to actually care for him. At that time I had no idea where he was coming from, or going to, but that our "out of the office" relationship was certainly going to be very different from the one at work. He told me I was the only person he felt he could trust, and then out of the blue told me he had a "mistress" or more correctly "a lady of ill repute". This was as the bill arrived, and I was gob-smacked. More so when he then casually said: "I'd like you to meet her. See what you think of her set up. Are you up for it?"I nodded, speechless."I thought you would be. Let's go and have a butchers."

'I expected that we'd go to some seedy sort of brothel. I couldn't have been more wrong. You know those lovely Queen Anne houses off Drayton Street? Well that's where we went. We were greeted by a gorgeous Madame, who told George that Serena was waiting for him in her usual boudoir, and as he left he said, "This is on me. Enjoy. See you in a couple of hours," and he beetled off through a side door. The Madame took me through double doors into this amazing room. It had a black ceiling with little lights looking like stars, huge vases of white lilies, and ladies like you've never seen before in various get-ups. Some of them were topless with revealing thongs leaving little to the imagination. They were lounging around on sofas with an assortment of happy clients, champagne flowing everywhere and also what looked like large glasses of martini. There were also a lot of rabbits, birds, beautiful slinky cats, and even a couple of monkeys. The whole set-up was bizarre, to say the least! Madame told me to enjoy myself as instructed by George, and left me to take it all in. Within seconds, a gorgeous, tall, blonde haired lady walked up to me, kissed me and said, "I'm Leila and I'm all yours. Why not have a cocktail and who knows what may happen?" The next two hours were a blur and went past far too quickly. I remember going to her boudoir where she massaged me, and did various other things but it didn't feel smutty. It was just great. It was weird, we chatted like old friends. It was as if we'd met at a party, and I wasn't married, and had no responsibilities.'

'I bet you've seen her since haven't you?' Dave asked.

'Yes, I have. It's like a drug. I just can't help it. I see her at least once a week in the early evening after work. And then the other evenings I have to work late, to save up the money to see her again and again. I'm trapped but I love it. Just recently I've told Shirley I've been away on business. That way I get to spend a whole night there, at a cost, but it's well worth it. Fortunately, as you've probably gathered, we're in the process of buying another factory up in Yorkshire, which I have to visit occasionally. So there's my excuse. But the strange thing is, Dave, I just don't feel guilty. Fulfilled, rather. She makes me feel as though I'm the only person in her life. Sometimes we even talk about marriage but I know that's just not on.'

'Has she got a sister?' Dave asked jokingly, 'anyway give me a bit more of what actually happens. You know, some of her tricks.'

'It's strange really, she does nothing unusual but just makes me feel loved. I can't go a whole week without seeing her. Weekends are hell, which is why my golf's gone off the boil.'

'You can say that again. Come on, you ought to be getting home and getting some beauty sleep. I wondered why you've looked so knackered recently.'

Later that week over Sunday lunch, when the family were all together, Shirley told them about Freddie, the parrot.

'Oh! I think that's really nice' said Angela, 'it'll be great fun having Freddie. He's getting on a bit though isn't he? Do you think Bristow will mind?' Bristow was their rather fat and smelly dachshund.

'I don't think so,' her mother replied, 'we'll just have to see. You don't mind do you darling?' she said to Keith.

'Not at all. If he reminds you and the girls of your vicar then that's fine. But don't expect me to have anything to do with him. I'm off to the golf course. See you all this evening.'

And so life went on in the Woodward household with Shirley taking delivery of Freddie, the children finishing their exams in June, and Keith "working late", "away on business", "just playing golf," or whatever excuse he could come up with to disguise his other life

The new vicar arrived and Shirley didn't take to him

immediately, instead she channelled all her love and affection into Freddie. Freddie was indeed a very handsome, green and red parrot, and he settled in very quickly. His repertoire of phrases was extensive and he often had the two children laughing out loud, although Keith was none too pleased if he was late for supper and Freddie would squawk,

'Late again, late again. Naughty Daddy. Naughty Daddy!'

'Bloody parrot! He's really getting on my nerves.'

Whereupon the children would say together in parrot fashion.

'Late again. Late again,' and burst out laughing.

But even Keith was upset a few days later when Shirley shouted to him upstairs,

'Keith, come down quickly. It's Freddie. I think he's dead.' And indeed he was.

It's easy to mock dead parrots after the infamous Monty Python sketch, but there was a genuine feeling of sadness in the Woodward family for the next couple of weeks.

Later, one morning at breakfast Shirley made an announcement.

'I can't cope without Freddie. I'm going to buy us another parrot. I know they're expensive but I'll shop around and see what I can find. My mind is made up so there's no point in trying to stop me.'

'Maybe you could find one on the Internet,' Angela suggested.

'Well I think you're mad,' Keith said, 'Freddie was special for you because of the Nicholls, and I honestly don't think anything could replace him. Also I think you should write and tell them the news.'

'Yes, I will, but only after I've got a replacement.'

'So where's the money coming from? I reckon they can cost up to £1,000, and your housekeeping certainly won't cover that,' Keith remarked unkindly.

'You may well snigger, but you actually started to like Freddie, so I'm determined that we should have another parrot. I promise I won't break the bank.'

'Okay. Do what you like darling. I know you will anyway. It's your housekeeping money, but make sure when you've made your purchase that there's still enough left to feed us all. Don't you agree girls?' He asked, staring at each of them in turn.

'I'm sure Mum will cope, and your belly will be kept full,' Tracy replied sarcastically.

'I agree,' said Angela, 'anyway let's face it, we'd all come to love Freddie, so I think Mum's doing the right thing.'

'Alright,' said Keith holding his hands in surrender, 'I'll look forward to seeing our new feathered friend this evening or whenever.'

After Keith had gone off to work, Shirley went on-line and began phoning round all the pet shops in the Bristol area. Parrots were certainly available, but at a price. The range was between £500 - £2000. Shirley had been thinking a couple of hundred quid at the most. After making over a dozen calls she gave up, and was resigned to the fact that they would never be able to afford another parrot. However, she had left her name with all the pet shops, in case something less expensive cropped up or someone couldn't cope and had decided to return their parrot. But she held out little hope, and was beginning to manage without Freddie, when late one morning the phone rang.

'Mrs. Woodward? It's Mister Green from Happy Pets here. You remember you phoned me a couple of weeks ago about a parrot? Well I've just had a four year old one brought in. It comes with a slight history, but it's a really lovely bird, and I think you ought to come and have a look.'

'Of course I will Mister Green. I'm on my way. One thing though. What do you mean it comes with a slight history? Is there something wrong with the bird ?' She enquired.

'No, not at all. Physically, it's a lovely specimen. It's just that it talks rather a lot. No more really than that.'

'That's not a worry. I'll see you shortly,' she replied.

'Good. I'll look forward to meeting you. I'm just off Ellison Road after the traffic lights on the left going out of town.'

'Oh, just one thing before I come out and see the parrot, what sort of price are we talking about, please?' she asked apprehensively.

'Don't worry. I remembered you were very worried about the cost. This parrot only cost me £100, so you can have it for £150.'

Shirley felt elated driving over to Happy Pets, but a bit concerned as to the state of a parrot costing only £150. Something must be seriously wrong at that price. Still, nothing ventured nothing gained, she thought as she hurried on her way, dodging in and out of the traffic, and driving much too fast.

She eventually arrived at Happy Pets in a high state of anticipation. She so wanted this parrot to be the right one.

She managed to find a parking space near the shop, and rushed in excitedly. It was absolutely full of animals and fish, ranging from puppies to kittens, rabbits to hamsters, budgerigars to goldfish. But no sign of any parrots.

'I've come about the parrot,' said Shirley to a nice looking, middle-aged man.

'Yes. Hello, you must be Mrs Woodward. I'm Bob the

owner and I keep my parrots in this room next door. Here let me show you the way,' he said negotiating his way through his shop and into the next door room. And what a sight. Against one wall was a large cage full of beautiful parrots of varying sizes and colours.

'My goodness,' said Shirley overwhelmed by the sheer colour of it all.

'Yes, parrots are my hobby and a very large part of my business. I sell to people the length and breadth of the country. They're pretty impressive aren't they? See this grey one here? That's a very rare African parrot and will sell for over £2000. And this small green one is worth nearly £1500.'

'Yes, they are very impressive. But which one is the one you were recommending for me?'

'Well, he's just here on this perch. See. He's very tame and very talkative.'

There, in the other corner, was the most beautiful parrot Shirley had ever seen. Its bright green and red colouring was absolutely breathtaking. She went up to it tentatively, making little whistling noises and was a little taken aback when it suddenly squawked in a very loud and clear voice:

'Hello Madame. Pretty Madame. Lovely Madame. Gorgeous Madame. Sweet Madame. Oh! Madame you are very pretty.'

'Oh, I am sorry Mrs Woodward. I didn't have a chance to tell you about Algernon.'

'Me, Algernon. You, pretty woman.'

Shirley was somewhat thrown by all this, and not a little flustered. She had to admit it was some parrot.

'Let me explain,' said Bob hurriedly. 'To be honest this parrot has picked up a lot of rather crude expressions from the previous owners, which is why they sold him to me.

He's only been here for a couple of days, and frankly his language is not as bad as I thought it was going to be. How did they put it? Oh yes. "Some of his chat might be bit blue." That's it. Of course it may be because he's now in a new place he's cleaned his act up a bit. But I can't really be sure, hence the price.'

'Lovely lady, pretty lady. Too good, too good,' Algernon screeched.

Shirley was both entranced and fascinated. Surely no language could be too blue for her family, for £150 the parrot was a bargain and Bob said that if it got out of hand he'd take it back and refund her.

'I love him,' said Shirley stroking the bird.

'And I love you, I love you. Pretty woman, pretty woman,' Algernon replied.

Shirley laughed and said to Bob,

'I'll take him. Whatever happens he's going to bring a lot of laughs with him and he is certainly the most beautiful parrot.'

'You're quite right. I don't think I've ever seen such a wonderful specimen. So if you can put up with the language you've got yourself a bargain.'

Shirley had brought her old cage. All cleaned out and ready for the journey home. There was no problem putting Algernon in it and Bob carried it out to Shirley's car.

'Thank you so much for calling me back,' said Shirley. 'I'm convinced Algernon's going to bring a lot of fun, laughter and happiness to our house.'

'I hope so,' Bob replied, 'and please don't forget if it doesn't work out I will take him back.' He shook Shirley's hand and waved to her as she drove off.

Shirley felt absolutely wonderful about her new

acquisition. She couldn't wait to get home and see what the family thought. She also wondered just how blue Algernon's language would be, away from his original home.

Once she'd arrived home, she parked the car in the drive and took Algernon into the front room where there was lots of light and the bird could watch passers-by on the street. It was really the family room so he would have lots of company. She took the cloth off the cage and Algernon looked round his new home.

'Pretty room. Pretty room. Good view. Good view. And you Madame, pretty Madame.'

Shirley took him out of his cage and left him perching on the top and went off to make a cup of tea. When she returned Algernon had his head under his wing, and was sleeping. Not for long.

'Pretty Madame, lovely Madame. No girls. Where the girls?'

Shirley was slightly worried by his reference to "girls." but then he quietened down and sat there looking very content and happy.

Shirley must have dozed off herself as the next thing she heard was her daughters coming home.

'Oh! Mum he's gorgeous,' Tracy said as she came into the room.

'Where did you get him from?' Angela asked as they both went up and stroked Algernon.

So she told them the story of why he was such a bargain, which made the girls giggle a lot.

'He's called Algernon and you must admit he's very handsome,' Shirley said.

'Hello girls. Hello girls. You nice new girls. And you're new girls. Algy find you nice men. Nice men for nice girls,' which had the girls doubled up giggling

'If that's as blue as it gets, I don't think you need to worry Mum,' said Angela, tears of laughter streaming down her face.

'Let's see if he enjoys the telly,' said Tracy.

So on went the television, and the three of them, plus Algernon all sat quietly watching the box, with their lovely new parrot gazing intently at the screen, and keeping quiet for a change. As usual Keith wasn't back for supper, so they decided to have it on their knees watching EastEnders with Algernon. Halfway through the programme they heard the front door open, and Keith came into the room.

'What on earth's going on?' he shouted. 'Why are you all watching the telly? I want my tea now, I've been busy all day and I'm very, very hungry!!' But Keith was interrupted by Algernon.

'Hello Keith. How are you? Nice to see you again. And where's your lovely Leila? Maybe Leila come here very soon. I hope so. I always liked Leila and you did too, didn't you Keith?'

'Who is on earth is Leila?!' Shirley and the girls asked in unison and none too softly!

MEMORY GAMES

It was a lovely summer's day - hot, with a few wispy clouds in the sky. The village of Lodsworth looked its best as Jean Willard made her way down The Street to the village shop, named the Lodsworth Larder, a successful enterprise conceived and run by the local community.

This was one of the reasons Jean had lived in the village for over fifty years. Everything was on her doorstep, including a pub - The Hollist Arms, a vibrant Village Hall situated on the recreation ground, and of course the beautiful village church of St Peter's, part of the parishes of Lickfold, Selham and Lodsworth itself. Although Jean was now in her eighties she was fit, active, and a popular character in the village. Her daughter, Penny and son-in-law, Rob, lived a few miles away in the village of Upperton, and they would often come over to make sure everything was alright. They had one son, Stephen, who had just left school and was waiting for his A Level results. He was the apple of Jean's eye, and spent lots of time at her pretty 18th century cottage, or driving her to one of the many local pubs for lunch. She always had so much to tell him of her past life, and he just loved her company. On this particular day he was due for lunch, which was why Jean was on her way to the village shop.

'Morning Mrs Willard,' Tacye, one of the shop's managers said, as she entered the premises. 'You haven't forgotten your shopping list I hope?'

'I don't think so, Tracy. That's not right is it? I know one of your admirers always calls you Tasty! Quite right too! I've got it. It's Tacye isn't it?'

'Quite right Mrs Willard.'

'Good! At least I haven't quite forgotten your name. But I have forgotten the name of the bakery in Haslemere where you get all your wonderful bread from. No, now I remember. "Bread of Heaven" and heavenly it is! Let me have a large white loaf please. Sadly that's all I can remember from my shopping list which I think I've left at home.' So saying she tipped the contents of her bag onto the counter. No shopping list.

'Wherever can it be? My memory really is getting bad isn't it?'

'Well, I'm afraid you do have a bit of a reputation for forgetting things. But it's only your short term memory isn't it? I have to say you always do really well at the Village Quiz. I love being in your team as we nearly always win.'

'That's as maybe, but I'd even forgotten that my grandson, Stephen, was coming over for lunch today. Thank goodness he phoned to check. You see I couldn't find my diary anywhere. It's all rather hopeless really.'

In fact, Jean and her family had been getting more and more worried about this forgetfulness. It had started shortly after her eightieth birthday and had become progressively worse. So much so that either Penny, or Rob, or Stephen, when he was at home, would phone every morning and evening to make sure everything was okay. Clearly it was all to do with old age creeping up on her, but nevertheless, Jean was beginning to feel frightened and vulnerable. She felt that people were laughing at her behind her back, or trying to catch her out. It was silly really, but it irked her, and, although her GP had given her some medication, things were no better, if anything, they were worse. It was all very sad, particularly as, on an intellectual level, she was still very much in control. Whilst Tacye in the shop had cheered her up, there was no denying that the questions asked at the Village Quiz were not of the same standard of those on Mastermind.

Jean had been married for fifty-six years, and she had met her husband, Robert, when they were both at Cambridge. Sadly he had died shortly before her eightieth birthday, which is when she thought her forgetfulness began. Now eighty-six, whilst she found her condition both annoying and frightening, she was able to look back on a very happy, contented life.

'I am no fool,' she said out loud as she walked back with her shopping to her little cottage just off the The Street, 'and I'd like to let all my friends know that. I'd like to do, or achieve, something memorable. If only I could silence my detractors, and make them realise that I have real substance, even though I may seem a bit batty. I'll talk to Stephen about it over lunch. I am sure between us we can come up with something. How I love that boy! He's so good to me.'

She opened the gate to her front garden and walked up the path.

Oh! No! She thought, I've now only gone and forgotten my front door key. I'm so stupid! Now, where did I hide the spare one? Oh, I can remember something! It's under a blue flowerpot in the greenhouse.

Leaving her shopping by the front door, she went round

the side of the house and into her greenhouse. But there was no key under the blue pot. She then remembered that Penny had said that it was an obvious place to hide a key, but where, thought Jean, had she suggested instead? She did have a mobile, which she took out, not really understanding it, but it did have four numbers on it - her daughter's, her son-in-law's, her grandson's and Rosie's, her faithful daily. She would try Rosie. She did not want Penny to know how hopeless she had become. Fortunately Rosie was in, and told her where it was now hidden.

'Now I really mustn't forget that must I?' she said aloud as she let herself in. As she bustled around the kitchen getting lunch ready for Stephen and herself, trying not to fall over her ancient black labrador, Hattie, she began to think of ways in which she could rediscover herself.

At midday her front doorbell rang, and there was Stephen, with a big bunch of flowers and a bottle of wine.

'Granny! Wonderful to see you! You're looking fantastic and, if I may say so, your green fingers have done excellent work in your front garden.'

'Thank you so much, Stephen. Yes, I have been busy but how observant you are. Come on in, and let's crack open that bottle. There's something I wanted to discuss with you over lunch.'

'Do I sense one of your naughty plots, Granny?'

'A plot, yes. But not naughty!' she replied grinning. 'Let's have our drinks in the garden. You have liver, your favourite, for lunch today darling.'

'But Granny!' Stephen exclaimed

'What?'

'It's nothing. I just wanted to know where you put the corkscrew. It's not in its usual place.' Liver, he thought -

yuck! His Granny had phoned earlier that morning to ask what he would like for lunch, and he had said "Anything, as long as it's not a piece of liver." Dear old thing, her memory is bad. Never mind, he would never let on and upset her.

Over their drinks in Jean's pretty walled garden, Stephen told her about his last four weeks at school, and how, at last, he had been awarded his cricket colours. He was planning to work on a local farm before trying for Oxford later in the year. Jean was very pleased he would be around, and unknown to him, was going to buy him a car if he got into Oxford.

After lunch and over a cup of steaming coffee, Stephen asked his Gran:

'What's this plot you're hatching? Should I be party to it, or is it one of yours that I might not approve of? What about that April Fool's trick you did on Libby Milling, or, worse still, the total chaos you caused at the Vicar's tea party? I also seem to remember something pretty humorous was perpetrated by you at last year's Village Fete.'

'No, no, no!! This needs to be much grander. As you know, my memory is sadly very poor. Already this week I managed to miss my bridge club, and completely forgot about Amanda Spence's drinks party yesterday. Fortunately she kindly called me to make sure I was alright and I hurried round to enjoy the fun. However nearly every day something goes wrong for me, and I know I'm getting the reputation of being a "batty old Granny". Somehow I need to prove to myself and all my friends that I'm not actually batty, and that I have a good brain. I've been thinking long and hard about exactly what to do, and now I have decided. I am going to try to get on that new programme on television,

"Ten Steps to Becoming A Millionaire", with that nice Harry Hewson.'

'Harry Henson, Gran.'

'Whatever! What do you think?'

'I think it's a great idea but do you think you could cope? Some of the questions are bound to be about TV soaps and pop music, which you know nothing about. Having said that, your general knowledge is first rate. Being a Granny might be an advantage actually, and help get you on the programme as one of their older contestants. Of course you'll have to go through the preliminary filtering process, before you actually get into the hot seat.'

Stephen poured some more wine for each of them, held up his glass and said,

'Good luck! Go for it. One of my friends' mothers was on it last year so I'll give her a call.' What about the "phone a friend"? Who would you call?'

'Easy. Andrew Mills at the pub. He's got a fantastic brain and dreams up the questions for the Village Quiz.'

'That's not a bad idea,' Stephen replied.

Later that afternoon as they both took Hattie for a walk through the village, it was agreed that Stephen would phone Mrs. Williams, his friend's mum, whose stepson Simon Channing just happened to work on the programme, and find out what the form was. For the moment this was their secret. If she was invited onto the programme then she would let all her friends know. She had told Stephen that nearly everyone she knew watched "Ten Steps To Becoming A Millionaire". To prove herself, she reckoned she needed to win a least £100,000, and promised not to blow it, if she was unsure of the next question.

Stephen agreed to phone her when he had spoken to Mrs

Williams. As he left later that afternoon, he said.

'Mum's the word, or in this case, Gran's the word. Bye Granny, thank you for a lovely lunch and I think your idea is brilliant. We'll show them.'

Mrs. Williams and her family were away on holiday for a couple of weeks, so life continued much as usual for Jean. And things didn't get any better. She lost her car keys, let her bridge partner down badly again through her forgetfulness, left a saucepan of milk heating up on the hob, and woke up from her afternoon nap to the sound of the smoke alarm. Every day something untoward occurred as a direct result of her poor memory. It was frustrating to say the least, and how she wished the Williams family had not gone away. She needed something positive to cling onto. Three weeks later her phone rang and it was Stephen.

'Gran, it's all settled. Our luck's in. Mrs Williams' stepson, Simon, thinks it's a cool idea and will be in touch with you shortly, once you've received your application form in the post, in the next couple of days. Let me know when it arrives, and I'll come over and help you fill it in. One last thing, if you get "into the chair", you'll be the oldest contestant they've ever had. So Simon, who's actually the assistant producer, will be looking out for your application. Exciting isn't it?'

'Oh rather! I can't wait,' and she put the phone down and did a little jig round her sitting room before tripping over her dog, and then, fortunately, collapsing into her favourite armchair, flushed with excitement.

Once Jean and Stephen had filled in the application form, things moved very quickly, as Simon Channing was particularly interested in having Jean on the programme. Partly because of her age but also, he felt, seeing her photograph, she looked "physically great", which Jean loved.

So before she'd really come to terms with the adventure ahead, she and Stephen found themselves at the BBC's studios at Shepherd's Bush. Simon Channing was there to greet them:

'You look lovely my dear, and now we need to get you into make-up.'

'Do you mind! I made an extra special effort this morning. I certainly don't need any more make-up thank you.'

Stephen, laughing, said, 'Granny, you have to be made up by a make-up artist for the TV cameras and particularly the studio lights.'

'Silly me! Of course I do! Let's go!'

This new BBC game show was considered harder than the original ITV one. Also, as stated, in the title, "Ten Steps To Becoming A Millionaire", there were only ten stages - £100, £1000, £2000, £5000, £10,000, £50,000, £100,000, £250,000, £500,000 and £1,000,000. With this programme you only had two lives. You could ask the audience and also phone a friend, but once a contestant answered incorrectly, he or she would lose everything. The show had been running for just over a year, with excellent ratings. Before the show began, Jean, with the other contestants, met up with Harry Henson, who she liked, which put her at her ease.

And then suddenly, it seemed to the nervous participants, the show was 'On Air'.

'Good evening, contestants and ladies and gentlemen in the audience. I think you all know the rules. To select our first contestant, a numbered list of five English cities will appear on the screens in front of each of you. All you have to do is put these cities in the right order, from north to south. Good luck!

'1 - Coventry 2 - Leicester 3 - Birmingham 4 - Worcester 5 - Peterborough.'

Jean was ultra-quick with her answer, rearranging the five cities featured on on her screen as follows: Leicester, Peterborough, Birmingham, Coventry and Worcester.'

'Well done Jean Willard from Sussex. You did it in 5.6 seconds, and only two others even managed to answer the question. So welcome to "Ten Steps To Becoming A Millionaire".

Jean got up nervously, and went over to Harry, who immediately gave her a big hug and whispered in her ear, 'Well done and you look fantastic.' He helped her up onto her chair, from where she was able to see Stephen up in the audience.

'I see you've spotted your grandson, Stephen. Was this his idea?'

'Actually it was mine. You see I've become very forgetful about silly things. You know – like losing the car keys, forgetting bridge sessions, and once I even left my poor dog Hattie down near the river and walked home on my own. Twenty minutes later there was a lot of indignant barking outside my front door. I'd not even noticed.'

'It would appear then, you've got something to prove. In a way.'

'Yes. It's silly of me but I'm convinced I've still got most of my marbles left.'

'We'll soon see won't we?' said Harry, and they both laughed.

'You seem very calm.' he said.

'It may appear that way to you, but the butterflies are having a field day!'

'Fine. I know you know the rules, but just let me remind you, and the audience, that you lose all your money if you answer a question incorrectly. But now, let play commence. Good luck. The first question is for £100. Which of these is a type of singer? Is it. 1 - Bravura. 2 - Pomodoro. 3 - Soprano. 4 - Orvieto?'

'Soprano.'

'Right, well done. Shall we carry straight on?'

'Yes please do.'

'Okay. Now for £1,000. In cricket what does LBW stand for? Is it. 1 - Low Before Wicket. 2 - Leg Before Wicket. 3 - Lost Behind Wicket. 4 - Leg Between Wicket?'

'My late husband was a keen cricketer, and he was always grumbling about dodgy LBW decisions. So it must be number two, Leg Before Wicket.'

'Quite right. Well done. Did you know at eighty-six you are our oldest contestant by some way. How do you manage to stay so young-looking?'

'Good genes, Harry. That's my excuse and also living life to the full.'

'Good answer. Now to question three, for £2,000. In chess, which of these is not a chess piece? 1 - Knight 2 - Castle. 3 - Cannon. 4 - Bishop? Please take your time.'

'It's a game I have never played but I often used to watch my father and mother playing. I can remember seeing a Castle definitely, and I think a Bishop and a Knight. So I'll go for number three - Cannon.'

'Are you sure?'

'As sure as I'll ever be.'

'Why not ask the audience?' Harry said helpfully.

'No. No. Number three - Cannon.'

'Absolutely correct. You now have £2,000. Have you

decided what to do with your winnings, if you win of course?' chuckled Harry.

'I'm definitely donating some of it to an Alzheimer's charity, for obvious reasons.' she said smiling, 'the rest, I really don't know. But please keep going otherwise my mind will wander.'

'OK. Question number four, for £5,000 - Who composed the music for the opera, The Marriage of Figaro.? Was it. 1 - Mozart. 2 - Rossini. 3 - Mendelsohn. 4 - Schumann?'

'That's a trick question because the opera is Italian so you would expect the answer to be Rossini. But no, it's number one - Mozart.'

'You seem fairly certain on that one?'

'Yes I am. I love opera and have seen the Marriage of Figaro many times. Lucky question really!'

'Well you've answered four out of the ten without any help. Well done. Do you want to carry on?'

'Oh yes, rather, I'm enjoying myself now'

'Good. On to question five, for £10,000. At the Olympic Games in London 2012 how many Gold medals did Great Britain win? Was it. 1 - 20, 2 - 23, 3 - 29 or 4 - 27?'

'Oh dear, that's a hard one,' exclaimed Jean. 'I'm not very good on sport, only tennis and cricket really. I'm sure it's not twenty or twenty three, as I do remember we did really well at the London Olympics. I enjoy watching it on TV as a spectacle, but I'm really not too good on the medal count, so I'll have to ask the audience.'

'OK, audience. Let's see if you can help Jean out. Hands on your buzzers. Go. Pretty encouraging result for you Jean. Ninety eight per cent say 29 gold medals.'

'Thank you so much everyone, especially as I thought it was 27. So, I'll go with them. Number three, 29 gold medals'

'Slight hiccup there, but you have made a very good decision Jean. 29 is correct! Only five more questions to take you to that magic million and you've still not phoned a friend. Who do you have in mind?'

'That was an easy choice. Andrew Mills, the landlord of my local pub, The Hollist Arms, in Lodsworth in West Sussex where I live. He sets some difficult questions for our annual Quiz so I'm confident he won't let me down. Fingers crossed of course!'

'Well Jean, we are now getting into big money. I can give you a cheque for £10,000 now or do you want to carry on? Remember, in "Ten Steps", if you make a mistake you lose everything.'

'Yes, it is a gamble, but that's what I'm here for,' she said smiling and looking up at Stephen, who smiled back and gave her a wave.

'OK then, for £50,000 and this is a difficult one, a bit of spelling. How are you at that?'

'We'll soon see, won't we?' she replied laughing.

'Nice one! This next one's horrid. Here's the cheque for £10,000. Do you want it?'

'No, keep it. Bring on the question.'

'Which of one of these words, in essence meaning a lack of courage, is correctly spelt? Is it. 1 - Pusillanimous. 2 - Pusilinammous. 3 - Pusillanimmous. 4 - Pussilanimous?'

'You're quite right Harry. Not a nice question to ask an old lady.' This comment had the audience roaring with laughter.

'Please take your time. Remember this is worth £50,000.'

'Less pressure please Harry. It's neither two, nor three, as "animmous" would only ever have one "m". So it's between one and four, and four doesn't seem right, so I'm pretty sure it's number one. No I'm sure I'm right, so I'll go for number one, and that's my final decision, and don't try and talk me out of it. Number one please.'

'Congratulations! You are absolutely right,' Harry said, with the audience applauding her effort.

'I'm so glad. I have to say it was a bit of a guess.'

'Well you guessed right. We'll keep going because you strike me as the type who would say, "let's be having you".'

'Yes I might, but please keep firing the questions.'

'Oh dear,' exclaimed Harry, 'this could quite easily catch you out unless you're into pop music, and remember it's for £100,000. Question seven, what was the Beatles first number one hit in the UK? Was it. 1 - Please Please Me. 2 - Love Me Do. 3 - From Me To You. 4 - I Wanna Hold Your Hand?'

'Tricky! But my son is a huge Beatles' fan and so am I!'

'Wow!! A Pop Granny!'

'Steady. I was a lot younger then, and went to see the Beatles live with my son in, I think 1964, at the Hammersmith Palais. For once my memory is going to serve me well, because they sang their first number one hit at that very concert that year! The song was "Please Please Me" so "Please Please Me" is my answer, or number one.'

'Good answer but you do stand to lose £50,000. Are you quite sure?'

'Absolutely positive. Number One.'

'And you're absolutely right. Well done and here's a cheque for £100,000. Why not take it while you're ahead?'

'No! No! No! I'm on a roll now, and I can still phone Andrew.'

'Yes, you're right. So for £250,000, which of these famous car hire companies used the phrase "We Try Harder" as part of their marketing campaign. Was it. 1 - Avis. 2 - Hertz.

3 - Budget. 4 - Capital?'

'It really must be my lucky day, because my son-in-law, Bob, used to work in advertising, and worked on a car hire account. I'll never forget their advertising slogan "We Try Harder", as they were always just behind the market leader, Hertz. So I'm going for number one, Avis. That's my final answer, Avis. Not Hertz. I'm positive. Don't stop me please, or I might change my mind. The answer is number one, Avis.'

'Now, Jean. It is all getting pretty serious. Did you ever think you would get this far?'

'Never! But don't try and talk me out of number one, Avis. Hertz doesn't sound right. Final, final answer, number one, Avis.'

'Well, Jean. I don't know what to say. I offered you £100,000 didn't I?'

'Oh no, don't tell me!' Jean cried out in anguish.

'Now I can offer you,' whereupon Harry paused for maximum effect, '£250,000. Many congratulations. Avis was right! I just can't believe this. You're now only two answers away from becoming our second ever millionaire. How are you feeling?'

'Great! Particularly happy that with only two questions left I can still phone my friend, Andrew. So, no pressure on him right now,' she said laughing.

'Quite right. I'm not going to bother to offer you a cheque for £250,000. You'll only refuse it, right?'

'You're learning, Harry,' she said, 'but I may change my mind after the next question.'

'Right then. On to question nine, for half a million pounds, a history one. When was the Battle of Bannockburn. Was it: 1-1311. 2-1315. 3-1314. 4-1313?'

'No idea whatsoever. I'm hopeless at history, I would probably get the wrong century! So it's clearly time to phone Andrew. Please.'

'Good decision,' said Harry, dialling Andrew's number.

'Hello and good evening Andrew! This is Harry Henson live on the programme, "Ten Steps To Becoming A Millionaire". You won't believe it. Your good friend, Jean Willard, is stuck on Question nine, with a chance to win £500,000. Can you help her?'

'I certainly hope so! Hi, Jean.'

'Hello Andrew. Good luck. If you are not sure of the answer I'll take the £250,000 and buy the village a few drinks at your pub.'

'Done!' Andrew replied, chuckling.

'So,' Harry said, 'please ask Andrew the question, and he only has fifteen seconds to answer.'

'OK! Now dear, sweet, Andrew. Please, what was the date of the Battle of Bannockburn? Was it: 1 -1311. 2 -1315. 3 -1314. 4 -1313?'

'Your fifteen seconds start now Andrew.' said Harry.

'Okay. Definitely not 1315 as it just doesn't look right nor do 1311 and 1313. And actually I do know it's 1314.'

'How sure are you, Andrew?'

'Very! I read that period of history at university, and the date of Bannockburn is firmly etched in my memory.'

'I'm afraid your fifteen seconds are up. So it's all down to you now Jean.'

'He sets some difficult questions at his Quiz night, but if it's "etched in his memory" let's go for it. I know that there are thousands of people out there watching who know the answer, and I'm just glad I've chosen Andrew.'

'I'll tell you what we'll do. If you go for it and you are

wrong, because you've been such a great competitor and not at all batty, we'll make a donation to your Alzheimer's charity of £10,000.'

'What a fantastic gesture. Thanks so much. Now I've got to go for it, haven't I? My mind has gone blank. Was it three or four he said?'

The whole audience shrieked, 'Three!!!!'

'We'll let that stand but strictly speaking no help's allowed except from me, and I would of course have said his answer was Three. So is Three the magic word?'

'Yes! Yes! Three. 1314 is my final answer,' said Jean holding her head in her hands.

'Why not reconsider and take the £250,000 on offer?'

'But I'm so near. I've got to go for 1314. Number three it is - 1314 and no going back, that is my final answer.'

'Oh Jean!'

'Don't do this to me Harry, please. My whole body is shaking, please put me out of my misery.'

'What can I say? You could have taken home £250,000,' he said, pausing again for effect, 'but – now instead it's £500,000. Andrew was right. The Battle of Bannockburn was 1314. Congratulations! You're halfway to becoming a Millionaire or, should I be very politically incorrect and say, Millionairess?'

'Oh my, oh my! I can't believe it. Thank you Andrew. About the new car I know you want. It's probably on, that's if I stay in. I just can't believe I've won £500,000. It's amazing.'

'Well, here's a cheque for half a million pounds,' Harry said above the continuous applause.

'You must be joking. Tonight is MY night. I'm not stopping now. No way. Let's go for the million, sorry Andrew but I've got to go for it. And Harry please don't try and talk me out of it.'

'I'm sorry, Jean, but aren't you getting carried away? £500,000 is yours and?' But Jean interjected and said,

'Sorry to interrupt, but let's have the final question and then discuss matters, if I haven't a clue.'

'OK! You're the boss. Question ten,' Harry said to a hushed audience. 'For one million pounds. Phew! I don't think I can stand the strain. How are you coping?'

'Not well, so please just ask the question.'

'Sorry. Okay. Final question for one million pounds. The Latin name for one of these flowers is Myosotis sylvatica. Which flower is it: 1- Snowdrop. 2 - Buttercup. 3 - Forget-Me-Not. 4 - Crocus?'

'I know it! I know it! It's got to be Forget-Me-Not!! After this evening it can't be anything else. The whole reason I'm here is because I forget everything. Day in. Day out. Someone up there loves me. Number Three, Forget-Me-Not. Final answer Harry Henson.'

'Please, please Jean, remember this is serious money. If you're wrong you lose absolutely everything.'

'It's fate and I know in my heart of hearts that I must go for it.'

'Jean Willard, rest assured, the audience here tonight, and the six million people watching will never forget you. 'You.... Are ....' he said pausing for maximum effect. 'Quite right!!! It is Forget-Me-Not!!! And your answer has just won you one million pounds. And here is your cheque!'

'No, please send it straight to my bank. I'm actually not sure where I left my handbag, and anyway if I take it home I'll probably forget where I left it!' Jean said howling with laughter, as tears welled up in her eyes. 'Fancy that,

Forget-Me-Not. I'll never forget tonight, ever. Thank you so much Harry, all of you in the audience for helping me out, Andrew for Bannockburn and my grandson Stephen for getting me on the show. I still can't believe what's just happened. I may be very forgetful, but I certainly won't forget tonight! Never! Ever!'

WHAT HO REEVES! A SPOOF

'What Ho! Reeves,' I said as my man placed a cup of tea on my bedside table and drew back the curtains, which he did every morning around nine o'clock.

'Good morning Sir. I trust you had a good evening at your club?' Reeves said suavely, opening the window a little bit more to get some fresh air into the room, to well and truly wake me up.

'Rather, Reeves. Absolutely topping. You remember my chum Russell Spinknoodle?'

'Yes, I believe I do, Sir. Isn't he your friend who changes cars every two to three months as the mood takes him?' Reeves replied in a rather diffident way.

'Quite, quite. Well he's actually just bought a brand new four wheel drive Mini Coopers S - in bright red, AND,' - I put the emphasis on the word AND to witness Reeves' reaction, 'it has a Union Jack on the roof! It's a spanking car, I drove it last night rather like Toad - poop pooping all the way along the Embankment.'

'Really Sir, I'm sure you must have had fun.'

Now reader, the only problem with Reeves is that he doesn't always follow my train of thought. He inevitably raises his eyebrows in dismay at my better ideas. So, I decided to tell him the good news when he brought in my lightly boiled egg, and after he had laid out my clothes. Moments later, Reeves glided into the room.

'Now listen here, Reeves, I've decided to buy a Mini exactly the same as Spinknoodle's, and please, you don't have to look at me like that. I've had my Golf for two years now, and I feel like a change. Bright red it will be, also with a Union Jack on the roof. Can't wait to see Lord Blenkinsopp's face when we arrive at Blenkin Hall this weekend. I know Auntie B will love it, and insist on a spin right away. So, Reeves, what do you think of my wheeze?'

'Sir. It's not quite what I would have thought a man of your standing would desire, but then again you are who you are, and after all it's your money.'

'Dash it Reeves, don't speak in riddles. I'll not be bullied out of it,' I retorted strongly.

'Very good, Sir. I'll go on the Internet and see if one to your specification is available. Bright red with a Union Jack on the roof, I see,' and he shimmied off.

'Good thinking, my man. Tootle Pip,' I said, once he'd left the room. I took the top off my four-and-half-minute egg. Lovely it was, too. One of a dozen recently given to me by my cousin Cecil from Sussex, who keeps a number of the rarer breeds of poultry. This egg, I surmised, was a Maran as it had that characteristic deep brown shell with sort of freckles on it, but I will witter on no more, tell you what my latest fad is, wine.

Not just the drinking of the fruity liquid. No, much more than just imbibing I have actually been attending evening classes twice a week and learning the history of wine, including, and of particular importance, the make-up of wines, be they shiraz or merlot, sauvignon or chardonnay.

It's actually a dashed good course, but you may be wondering why I am wasting two evenings a week learning about wine when I could be coving at my club with my fellow bounders. Simple - it all boils down to my allowance. Now Auntie B and I get on like a house on fire and she gives me a very decent monthly bung which, along with my family trust income, means I really don't have to work at all. This makes one's life dashed bearable. Nevertheless, dear Auntie B felt that it was high time for me to be doing something worthwhile, or at least become an expert on something specific rather than, as she so succinctly put it - "swanning around doing precisely nothing for anyone except yourself". Bit hard wouldn't you agree? Anyway, things got a bit sticky on my dear Auntie B's allowance front, when Stinker Searle and I spent a night in clink following an excellent dinner and snooker session at Droons - my club. Something to do with pinching a policeman's helmet and promenading down The Mall quaffing bottles of champagne. I don't remember much about it, except being hauled up before the Magistrates' Court the next morning in front of Lady Wainwright, who just happens to make up a four at bridge with Auntie B. Reeves turned up and paid the fine but the damage was done. Auntie B was round at my place promptly at midday, refused a glass of sherry twice, most unusual for her, and proceeded to lecture me in no uncertain manner. And this, briefly, is what she said and why I'm studying wine.

'Now listen carefully young Harry Hooter, your recent jaunts have now gone too far.'

'But Auntie...'

'No interruptions please, where are your manners? I am talking and you will listen to me and if you don't I'll cut you off for good - without a penny . What you need is some discipline in your life. It would be nice if a young gal could quieten you down, but your record with women is poor to say the least. How many times have you been engaged Harry?'

'I really don't see...' I replied, only to be forcibly interrupted.

'Answer the question please,' she snapped.

'Six actually, but there were always extenuating circumstances,' I said, standing up for the Hooter name.

'Extenuating circumstances. Absolute twaddle, more likely the poor gals soon realised what a worthless and lazy bounder you really are. Enough of that and yes, Reeves, I think I'll now take you up on that glass of sherry. Nothing though for Harry. He needs to listen to me.'

You may be wondering why Reeves was with us. Well, actually he is the main reason my Aunt continues to support me. She said that without him I'd be a famously tragic figure. Reeves shimmied, as his his wont, into the room with a glass of sherry wine on a silver salver and my Aunt continued:

'One thing I know you enjoy is imbibing, and I'm not about to be hypocritical. Your knowledge of wine when I have been in your presence at various house parties has been appalling. You can barely tell the difference between a claret and a burgundy, or a sauvignon from a chardonnay. You were particularly embarrassing at the Curzons earlier this year when my cousin Charles quizzed you about the claret, and all you could say was; "Quite delicious. I've always liked red wine." Frankly, Harry, that was quite pathetic. As you know Lord Blenkinsopp, who is the owner of one of the best cellars in the country, is giving his annual summer house party at Blenkin Hall at the end of June. That gives you just three months to learn everything you need to know about wine. I have discussed this with Lord Blenkinsopp and on the Saturday night, you will have to correctly identify three French wines, and a port which we will be drinking with our dinner. If you get all four correct I will raise your allowance by between 10% to 20%; depending on my mood; three wines right, it stays the same, only two, and it goes down 20%, only one, down 25% and none at all, no allowance. I've already enrolled you on the Rothschild Fine Wine course, which also includes two lectures on port. Incidentally, it starts this evening and carries on twice a week for three months. Thank you for the sherry Reeves, and please ensure his attendance. There is a lot at stake. Cheerio, Harry, and don't look so glum. You should at least get the port right - after all, you drink enough of it by the look of your Droon's bill last month.' So saying she got up, and Reeves saw her to the door.

'What did you make of all that, Reeves?' I asked as he came back into the room.

'Quite a task, Sir. I suggest we buy a book on wine now and you can read through it as quickly as you can before this evening. You don't want to appear too hopeless, do you?' I am sure I saw a slight smirk on his face, certainly a raised eyebrow.

So that's about it. I have been attending the course for its full three months, and I have one more lecture before Lord Blenkinsopp's house-party at the weekend. I was hopelessly unprepared, even though my man Reeves had been a real brick helping me with my homework and doing plenty of blind tastings with me. Not an exercise I enjoyed. All the sniffing, swilling and disgustingly - spitting! Why can't a chap take a decent gulp instead of all that mumbo-jumbo of "tasting like pineapple with a touch of citrus and grass?" If it was meant to taste like that, then why hadn't somebody bottled it and called it Pineapple Citgra Green Cordial? Still, I had learnt a lot and was having my last lecture on port that very evening. Auntie B was right. Port hadn't proved too difficult, so the worst possible scenario would be 25% off my allowance. Heigh Ho!

'Ah! Reeves,' I said as he sashayed, as only he can, into the room to take away my breakfast tray. 'Any joy on the Mini front?'

'Well, Sir,' he replied demurely, 'it would appear that there has been a cancellation on a Mini Cooper S, with 4 wheel drive but with the Cross of St George on the roof. Maybe the Cross of St George will hopefully put you off a trifle?'

'Certainly not, Reeves. Top-hole! It sounds absolutely spiffing. When's it available?'

'Not until after the weekend I'm afraid, Sir'

'Never mind. I can wait. I'm so excited. Thank you so much Reeves.'

'Yes Sir. Will that be all, Sir?'

'Rather.'

I didn't have anything on that day, as I had decided to miss out on Droons monthly lobster luncheon, in favour of catching up on my reading for this evening's discourse on port.

Later, on my way to the Rothschild lecture, I bumped into Rosie Somerset in the Strand.

'What Ho! Rosie. How the devil are you?' I asked and kissed her gently on both cheeks. Rosie I'd known for many years, and she had always been a good chum, but just a chum, although sadly I had not seen her for a while. And how she had blossomed. She looked gorgeous and she quite bowled me over.

'Hi Harry! I'm fine. I've just come back from doing an art course in Florence. It was super. Now I'm off to hear my Uncle Bertie's lecture on port. He's my very favourite man, and I'm looking forward to his lecture. Apparently, he's one of the leading authorities on port in this country. Do you know Bertie Ballin?'

'Rather. As a matter of fact, I'm off to see him myself, as I've been attending all the Rothschild lectures for the past three months.'

'I am surprised, Harry. It's quite a tough course apparently, and I thought you spent most of your time at the races or at your club.'

'Do you mind? Come, take my arm. We'll saunter over to the final lecture and I'll tell you what I've been up to.'

Rosie was a very attentive listener, and I was delighted when she told me she had also been invited to Blenkin Hall for the weekend.

'Excellent,' I replied, 'an added incentive for me to do well. If I get at least two correct will you dine with me next week, Rosie?'

'Harry, don't be silly,' she replied, blushing slightly and looking prettier by the minute. 'You can take me out any time.'

'Oh heck! Can I? Oh gosh! How wonderful!' By which time I think I was also blushing, as she had certainly made my day.

There had originally been fifty of us on the course but a few had fallen by the wayside, and we were now down to thirty. After Rosie had had a few words with her uncle she came and sat next to me.

'Following our session earlier this week,' Bertie began, 'you will have realised that there are not as many outstanding ports as there are wines, for reasons we have covered. For the purpose of today's final selection I have chosen just eight, four of which are undoubtedly the best available today. So please listen carefully and then we will begin the tasting.'

I actually found it quite hard to concentrate with Rosie at my side, but by the end of the lecture I was quite chuffed to have got four out of eight right. The next best managed only got three. There was hope for me yet.

On the way out I bid goodbye to Bertie and Rosie.

'Listen Harry.' said Bertie, 'I know Lord Blenkinsopp quite well, and I believe your fellow guests will expect him to serve up a Taylor's '27, because of its cachet of being over 90 years old. However, I think he will go for the Croft '55 which is a smoother port, in fact, one of the ones you got wrong. So if you don't recognise it, plump for Croft '55 and good luck!' With that Bertie shook my hand and Rosie kissed me goodbye, whispering in my ear.

'Looking forward to Friday, Harry.'

There was definitely a spring in my step as I set off up the Strand to Droons. I had arranged to dine there with Bas Bootle, as he was a complete wine buff. During dinner, when we drank a Montrachet, a Lafite, a Sauternes and some port, he told me what to expect.

'If I read Lord Blenkinsopp correctly you are almost certain to have a Château d' Yquem as your pudding wine, and I agree with Bertie Ballin, a Croft '55 for your port. Anyway you managed to get the port and the white right tonight. Just one more and your allowance is secure. Come on, let's go and play snooker.'

During the second frame I asked Bas if he knew Rosie Somerset, explaining I'd just bumped into her earlier that evening, and thought her an absolute corker.

'A cracker, Harry. A real cracker. I know her brother, Michael very well, and apparently she had all the aristocracy in Florence, such as they are, after her, but she spurned them all. Probably waiting for someone like you to come along,' he said, laughing.

'Well why not?' I retorted, 'Heck, if I get all four right on Saturday, I'll be quite a good catch.'

'No chance. I hate to say it, but you're not in her league. I doubt she'd ever go out to dinner with you.'

'Fifty quid she will,' I said confidently.

'OK, you're on,' he replied as we shook on it. Not a bad way for me to earn fifty quid I thought smugly, as I potted the black and won the second frame.

On the way home that night I thought long and hard about Rosie Somerset. She really had made quite an impression on meself, what! I realised that if I was able to get all four wines correct, she would think of me as an above average sort of cove. That, and the fact that my allowance would go up by 10%-20%, made me even more determined. I had to admit, though, that I'd never identified all four wines correctly before. My best was only ever two. I had just two days left before Friday afternoon and I spent them immersed in books, punctuated with visits to fine wine emporia, such as Berry Brothers, to purchase and taste.

Later that night, Reeves manifested himself in my drawing room where I was poring over my lecture notes.

'Ahem,' he coughed politely, 'did Sir realise it was past two o'clock?'

'Really Reeves, have you been waiting up for me?' I

replied in a tired tone.

'Of course Sir. I have been making myself cups of coffee for the past three hours to keep awake. If you don't mind me saying so, Sir, you really ought to get some sleep before your wine session at J.T.Davies at midday tomorrow.'

'Quite right Reeves. Tootle pip, night night and all that. I'll just finish this chapter and then off to Bedfordshire.'

I had arranged a final tasting at my great chum, Mickey Snooks-Davies's house in Kent. He was going to provide twelve different French wines and some ports, to taste similar to the ones he believed Lord Blenkinsopp might give us, realising, rightly, that he would only serve the best.

Mickey's family had been in the wine business for well over a hundred years, and I was quite excited when I saw all the wines and ports with their labels obscured, with a card face down by each bottle. Whilst we had been taught exactly how to taste at the Rothschild lectures, Mickey felt that the key area was in the bouquet of the wine. He also suggested that I take four different brand new glasses with me to Blenkin Hall.

'You need to take a couple of litres of Evian with you and place the glasses in a basinful of the mineral water in your room,' Mickey said, 'leave them for half an hour, and then on no account dry them. Just let them drain on a piece of plain glass. Then take them down with you to dinner, but do not let them out of your sight. That way at least your nose will only pick up the wine's bouquet, rather than mixing it with the smell of washing up liquid, or worse still that "Finish" stuff people use in dishwashers. I've had it all packed up for you, so please take it with you when you leave.'

'Thank you so much, Mickey,' I said, 'every little bit helps.

What!'

'Good, then let's taste.'

I was really shocking, or as my old beak at Eton used to say, "not even that good". I was correct on two - one white, a sauternes and, one port, the Croft '55. That one was encouraging after what Bertie Ballin had said.

Mickey, who knew Lord Blenkinsopp and sometimes supplied his wines, felt that the white and the red would be obscure and therefore very difficult, but that the pudding wine and port would be more straightforward, primarily through lack of choice.

'Once the wine is poured, just leave it to settle for over thirty seconds and then swirl it around the glass at least ten times. After this, plunge your nose in for a good sniff or two or three, prior to tasting. Remember also to chew a biscuit between each course. Good luck!'

'Thanks so much. I'll try to remember all your wonderful advice.' I had actually taken quite a few notes to remind me of his "pearls of wisdom".

'Sorry Harry, one last thing, no cigars the night before, don't drink anything for lunch on Saturday and certainly don't brush your teeth before dinner however bad your breath is,' Mickey laughed as he accompanied me out to my car.

'Cheerio and again good luck. Remember how important the bouquet of the wine is. Byeee!'

I thought I would stay in that night. I was a bit nervous and not hungry at all, although Reeves did rustle up a fluffy omelette which I accompanied with a glass of water, as a way of resting my taste buds for Saturday evening's "trial by wine".

Motoring down the following afternoon, I quizzed Reeves

on my pending Mini Cooper S with the St George's Cross.

'Come on Reeves. Don't be such a stick in the mud. A Mini Cooper S has to be my kind of motor - a bit of pace and dash. What do you say?'

'Well, Sir. Far be it for me to be judgmental on your preference in motors, but I feel that something a little less flamboyant might be more appropriate. However, you are the final arbiter of what is correct for a man of your standing.'

'Now, Reeves, be blunt. Yes or no?' I said hurriedly, knowing what the answer would be.

'No, and I will say no more on the matter Sir,' Reeves replied haughtily.

I had this knack of getting under Reeves's skin, and once I had, there was no turning back. A Mini Cooper S, with all the extras, albeit vulgar in Reeves's opinion, it would be just dandy for me. It was all done and dusted, and I was particularly relishing the thought of Reeves accompanying me in my new motor. It would be a delight to observe his discomfort.

'I think we take the first right after the Snooty Fox as we leave Tetbury, if my memory serves me well. Yes Reeves?'

'If you say so, Sir.'

'And then we motor for a few miles and take the turning by St Augustine's church towards Edgeworth. Blenkin Hall is about a quarter of a mile along there on the right.'

'If you say so, Sir.'

By now Reeves had taken the hump, and all because of a Mini Cooper S. Well dash it, I wasn't going to have to put up with it much longer as Blenkin Hall hoved into view.

'What a spiffing pile, don't you know Reeves?'

'I could not agree with you more Sir, a magnificent

edifice,' he replied casually.

'Do look Reeves. Isn't that a Mini Cooper S parked by the front door?'

'It may appear so, Sir, but Minis are not my speciality.'

'Never mind, Reeves. Wow! How exciting! I wonder who it belongs to?'

'It would appear that the owner is Sir Tony Wilmott-Woolley who is, as we speak, walking down the front step with, I believe, Rosie Somerset. He is probably taking her for a spin.'

I hooted the horn and wound down the window.

'What Ho! Rosie. And Tony, how are you? Great car. I'm picking one up on Monday. Where are you off to?' I asked jealously.

'Tony's taking me to the George and Dragon near Tetbury. See you later,' she said as Tony solicitously opened the door for her.

'Dash it Reeves, if only I'd purchased my new car this weekend. She's not going to be interested in me now, with that rich and titled cove Tony around.'

'With the greatest respect, Sir, if you think you are going to win a lady's hand through a popular make of car, that might be construed as a bit naïve,' Reeves replied as he started unloading our luggage.

'I say, Reeves, that was a bit below the belt.'

'You asked for my opinion, Mr Hooter, and you have it. I will ring the bell and hopefully we will be directed to our quarters.'

Frankly, reader, I never like it when Reeves gets into one of his moods. But I had a lot at stake over the weekend, and I was not prepared to listen to Reeves whingeing about my new motor, or his observations about Rosie Somerset.

As we emerged from the car, Lord Blenkinsopp and Auntie B welcomed us.

'Wonderful to see you Harry!' said his lordship, 'we have quite a gathering here this weekend. You know all of them and everyone is eagerly looking forward to your Aunt's little wager tomorrow night. I hear you have put in quite a lot of training.'

'Well, yes Sir, I have,' I muttered as a young cove flew out of the front door and landed at my feet. It was young Horace Harmsworth, my impertinent Godson and bête noire.

'Hello, Harry. I need to earn another fifty quid to buy myself a digital camera. What can I do for you? Clean your car, your shoes, whatever?' he asked breathlessly.

'Now listen here, young Horace, this is an important weekend for me, and I certainly don't want you interfering with things. Talk to me on Sunday morning when I've done my wine tasting, but for the moment keep out of my sight,' I said strongly.

'But Harry....'

'No buts. Unless you have something useful to say, please keep your distance.'

Whereupon Reeves and I entered the Hall, found our rooms and Reeves unpacked my bags.

'Please be careful with those glasses, Reeves. It could be your livelihood at stake if I mess this up.'

'Very good Sir. When shall we execute the cleansing of the glasses as per Mr Davies's instructions?'

'Tomorrow evening shortly before dinner. Nothing must be allowed to interfere with this preparation. Also please do make sure you keep young Horace well away from me. He is an impertinent young bounder, with a very aggravating manner.'

I spent the remainder of the afternoon and early evening meeting the rest of the house party, which in total numbered fifteen people. Gussie Flack-Tootle and his fiancée, Rowena Rawlings, were amongst the guests, and it was good to see young Gussie who is a proper cove and a fellow member of Droons. I vaguely knew everyone else but I was not on good form that night, retiring early with the thoughts of tomorrow's tasting etched in my mind. Reeves's mood was no better and when he brought me my late night tipple, there was a certain froideur in the air .

'Thank you Reeves for keeping young Horace out of my sight. I just can't cope with him at the moment,' I said glumly.

'If you do not mind my saying so, you need a good night's sleep and lots of fresh air tomorrow to liven up your taste buds.'

'Thank you, Reeves.'

He was right as usual and I was soon in the land of nod..

I had arranged to meet Rosie in the garden after breakfast, for a stroll around the arboretum. So, imagine my surprise when I saw her in her tennis gear.

'I'm most frightfully sorry, Harry, but after you had retired so early, I was asked by Tony to make up a four for tennis. Please forgive me,' she said as she ran off towards the tennis court. My initial reaction was "poor form" but I was too engrossed in the evening's affairs to worry over much, although it looked as if old Tony was "well in" there. Anyway, good luck to him for trying, I thought. Of supreme importance to me was tonight's dinner. Therefore after luncheon where everyone, except me, was very jolly, I found a deck chair and sat down beside the lake with a book, to help calm my nerves.

After a few moments, Auntie B sailed into view.

'Come on, Harry. You're not your usual jocular self. This house party needs a fool like you and yet so far you've done nothing to entertain the troops.'

'How can I, Auntie B? You've set me a hard task and I intend to go through with it. Not only to secure my allowance but to increase it,' I replied with some venom.

'Harry, there's no way you will win. I set you this task because I think you need a good kick up the backside. I believe I'm already giving you too much, you need to supplement your allowance, maybe by getting a job, rather than wasting your time at Droons and going to endless house parties'

'Thank you so much, dear Auntie B, for your kind consideration,' I replied sarcastically.

'Well, frankly, Harry, I'm bored of everyone saying how much I spoil you. At least I've set you a challenge to prove yourself,' she said waving goodbye and saying she was looking forward to the evening ahead.

My mood really couldn't have been much worse. I could hear the other guests having a great time playing croquet and tennis. Doubtless Tony was making a play for young Rosie. So I retired to my room in a huff and sought the relief of sleep. Imagine my surprise and concern when I awoke to find Reeves with young Horace at the end of my bed.

'Sorry Reeves but what on earth have you got that young bounder in my room for? Get him out at once,' I exclaimed.

'Excuse me, Sir.' whined Horace, 'I've got something that I think might be of interest to you later this evening. It is to do with the wines, but I want fifty quid up front before I say any more.'

'Sir,' intoned Reeves, 'I think you should hear him out.'

'Very well Horace, carry on. We'll see about the fifty pounds later. Now spit out your info.'

'It's like this,' Horace said. 'I was down in the kitchen minding my own business getting rid of my chewing gum in the pedal-bin thingy when, as I opened it, I saw a couple of wine labels. Now, I believe you have quite an important evening ahead of you, Sir.'

'Cut the cheek Horace! What have you in mind?'

'Well, for fifty quid, I'll tell you what the labels said, if I can remember.'

'Didn't you bring them with you, you buffoon?' I said nonplussed.

'I couldn't. Cook saw me looking at them and banged down the lid and told me to scarper - sharpish,' Horace replied.

'So?' said I quizzically, 'Are you quite sure you can remember exactly what you saw for this fifty quid?'

'Positive. We're studying Charlemagne in history at Stowe, and one label read 'Corton Charlemagne '96.' But before I continue, can I please see the colour of your money?'

'Reeves, please fetch my wallet. It's on the dresser.'

By now I was sitting bolt upright, realising that a mere fifty smackers could very nearly secure my allowance. If the other label was the claret and I could guess the port right, then I was there!

'Second thoughts, dear Godfather,' the wretched child remarked, 'if I'm not mistaken, there is, according to everyone here at Blenkin Hall, quite a lot at stake for you tonight. Yes?'

'Yes, there is, you nasty pipsqueak. Come on tell me what the other label was.'

'Hundred quid minimum for them both,' he replied.

'Okay, Reeves show him the money,' I said. Daylight robbery suddenly seemed like a good investment.

'I remember the other label because our local pub at home is called the White Horse and I thought what a strange name for a wine - Cheval Blanc.'

'Yes, okay but what year, what year?' I asked frantically.

'It was either '55 or '59. But you could always look it up, as I'm sure my uncle would only serve the best.'

'Very perspicacious, young man,' said Reeves, as he went to the bureau and took out my "bible". Reeves leafed through it.

'It says here, sir, that the '59 is one of the finest clarets ever produced, and has not been bettered since.'

'Come here, young Horace. Here is your hundred quid and "mum's the word", otherwise I'll thrash the living daylights out of you,' I said as I handed over five twenty pound notes.

'Don't worry, sir. Our family motto is "Aut Mors Aut Victoria" and my word is my bond. Honest, and thanks for the cash. Tootle pip, as you would say,' and he beat a hasty retreat.

'What do you think, Reeves? Should we believe him, or has he decided to make me a real chump tonight and dump me in the proverbial?'

'No sir. The boy was obviously telling the truth. He would never have been able to give you those names unless he had seen them. He is, with respect, not the brightest candle in the candlelabra. Although I've always quite liked the lad. It could be a scam, but I very much doubt it.'

'You are right, Reeves. Please draw my bath, and I'll then get dressed for dinner. Also, please ensure you put out the correct dinner jacket tonight. Thank you.' I was very attached to my old dinner jacket, which Reeves thought had seen better days. This was another one of his old gripes, as clearly Reeves and I were going through the motions. He was still upset about the Mini Cooper S as I was, in a way, since Tony Wilmott-Woolley had clearly impressed Rosie with his motor - or so I thought.

Reeves had done his stuff with the glasses. The assembled house party was quite surprised when I bowled up for cocktails with my man carrying four glasses on a silver tray.

'Harry, old chap,' said Lord Blenkinsopp, eyeing the silver tray with some apprehension. 'Are my crystal glasses not good enough for you?'

'With the greatest of respect, I was advised to bring my own drinking vessels. I trust you are not offended?'

'Of course not, old chap. Delighted you're taking it so seriously, what? So, Beatrice, are you impressed?' he said, turning towards my Auntie B.

'I certainly am. Well done, Harry, so far so good.'

I declined cocktails and kept away from the smokers and just wished that "dinner was served".

'Dinner is served, your Lordship,' Jeavors, their old butler, shortly intoned.

I escorted Lady Blenkinsopp into dinner and was pleased to find I was sitting next to her and Rosie Somerset, which was spiffing!. Once we had all taken our places our host, Lord Blenkinsopp, called for silence as he arose and said:

'I think we all know this is an important evening for young Harry Hooter. Please do not let his "trial by wine" spoil it. All the wines and port have been decanted, and I have the names on the cards in my pocket. I know, Lord Melford, that you are quite a wine buff and your column in the Spectator is excellent, but please don't you or anyone else give the game away. I am certain you will all enjoy this evening's fare, except perhaps young Harry. Please serve the wine, Jeavors, and good luck Harry!' he said with a twinkle in his eye.

'Harry, are you alright? Rosie asked.'You look quite pale.'

'Fine, fine thank you. Top-hole. After all I've not got much to lose, have I?'

'Oh, I am sorry, silly old me,' she said, lightly touching my hand.

I have to get this right I thought, nibbling at one of the biscuits Jeavors had kindly laid at my place. The first course was scallops, but I needed to taste the white as soon as I could, and before I started my food parcel. All eyes were on me as Jeavors stood at my side pouring the deep yellow white wine into one of my own wonderfully squeaky clean glasses. I swallowed my biscuit, brushed away the crumbs from my mouth, took a deep breath and exhaled lightly. I rolled the liquid around the glass a dozen times, plunged my nose in and took in the wonderful bouquet, nearly choking with nerves. I had been placed at the top of the table and had Jeavors standing to my right with a spittoon. I took a small mouthful, swilled it around my mouth for a few seconds and then spat it out. The tension was unbearable.

'Come on, Hooter,' said Toby, 'you're clueless and you've no idea have you?' he said, laughing along with the rest of his chums.

'Patience please,' said Lord Blenkinsopp, 'take your time Harry.'

I felt a bit of a fraud, as it tasted like Chablis rather than Corton Charlemagne '96, which I had enjoyed once before. To join in the spirit of things and relax everyone, including myself, I just said.

'It's certainly a wine of distinction.'

'Bravo!' said Gussie, 'even I'd spotted that.'

'It is a '96 Corton of some variety, I think, but I'm not positive.'

I went through all the rigmarole again, and finally and triumphantly exclaimed

'By Jove, I've got it. It's a Corton Charlemagne '96. Right, Lord Blenkinsopp?'

'Absolutely right. Well done, Harry,' he exclaimed as a quiet ripple of applause went round the table.

'One down and three to go,' said my Auntie B smiling and dinner commenced.

I picked at my scallops not wishing to aggravate my taste buds and talked quietly to Lady Blenkinsopp and Rosie. Two better companions a fellow could not have had in those circumstances.

When the fillet of beef arrived Jeavors poured me a glass of rich-looking red wine. I took a long time taking in its bouquet and cogitating over its provenance. Yet again I took in the bouquet, swirled and swirled and spat at least three times before saying:

'Well again his Lordship has done us proud. This is a very fine claret with an excellent pedigree. I sense it's not from the Medoc region as the bouquet or flavour is not similar to say, a Lafite or Morgon. So, if it's not a Medoc it must be one of the very fine wines from further inland,' I said pausing, 'say Pomerol or St Emilion, and knowing our host's prediliction to offer up only the best, it's either Petrus or Cheval Blanc. Somehow I don't believe it's Petrus as it hasn't the right intensity. No blackberry, what! So I'm going to plump for ... yes ... I declare it's.... Château Cheval Blanc 1959. By Jove what a treat!'

'Silly Hooter. Blanc is the french lingo for white, can't you see this is a red. You're losing your grip old man. I mean really!' said Tony triumphantly.

'Shut up Tony!' Lord Blenkinsopp said, 'Harry is absolutely spot on. Well done. How on earth did you know that?' he asked curiously, staring down the table. I tried to look cool, and answered:

'It was a wine we tasted during the Rothschild lectures - although not a '59, rather I believe it was a younger vintage, '66. This is so much better. Thank you. It made a big impression on me then. It's a Premier Grand Cru, a class act, and very decent of you to serve it. I trust it's not wasted on a heathen like Tony.'

'Quite so Harry!' smiled Lord Blenkinsopp as everyone burst out laughing.

'I am impressed. Two out of four. Well done,' Rosie said, 'do you think you can manage all four?'

'I just don't know. But what I do know is young Tony has made a hit with you!' I stated unequivocally.

'That nincompoop! You must be joking. His family is appalling and his taste in cars even worse.'

I was aghast. I couldn't believe my luck. But she had more to say......

'I felt bad about the arboretum this morning, and then when I came back from tennis, I heard you had retired to bed. Maybe we could meet tomorrow instead, and play some tennis or croquet in the afternoon?' she asked.

'Top-hole!' I enthused. 'Rather, I m..m..mean, yes, wonderful idea.' And before I knew it, the pudding wine was being poured to complement the raspberry dish set before me. Now I was certainly in uncharted territory and really needed to pay attention.

'Good luck with this one, Harry' Lord Blenkinsopp bellowed from his end of the table, obviously well clareted up. 'Not an easy one at all, what?'

Heck, I thought. He was right. Definitely d'Yquem, but what year? I thought it was going to be an '80, which was one of the best ever, but this was a year I knew but it just didn't taste right.

'Definitely a Château d'Yquem, Lord Blenkinsopp probably an '80s vintage but what year it is, I just don't know. '80 is the one I know, and now I'm beginning to sound like someone on some sort of quiz show on the telly, what?!'

I tasted again and again and was convinced it was not an '80. But what exactly was it? I did remember that '83 was a classic year for sauternes, but would that necessarily apply to this d'Yquem, I wondered.

'I'm going to go for the '83. It's a Château d'Yquem '83,' I stated finally.

'Are you sure, quite sure?' said Lord Blenkinsopp.

'Categorically. Yes, I think, if you know what I mean. I'll go for it. Château d'Yquem '83.'

'Right again. You are doing brilliantly, young Harry,' said Lord Blenkinsopp.

'Three out of three,' Auntie B said, 'and your allowance is secured. I'm very impressed, Harry. You must have worked very hard. Good luck with the port.'

Just at that moment, young Horace came bounding into the dining room, hopefully, just to say goodnight to his parents, but still, my heart skipped a beat. He came up to my end of the table, gave me a huge wink and said.

'Thanks for the money, Harry. Very generous of you,' and my heart stopped beating completely. He was going to give me away. I knew it.

'Rather over-generous, if you don't mind me saying so, but your car will look spick and span inside and out before luncheon tomorrow.' So saying he tootled off.

'What was all that about?' enquired Lady Blenkinsopp.

'Nothing really. He's my Godson, you see. And I spoil him,' hoping this would shut her up. Thankfully, it did.

Finally we arrived at the port. It seemed to me that I was running a marathon with the finishing post just about in sight, I vainly hoped.

'So, Harry. You are nearly there aren't you?' enquired Lady Blenkinsopp, 'do you think it is going to be a Dow, Croft or Taylors? My husband is partial to all three.'

'Well, Lady Blenkinsopp, knowing his Lordship's exemplary taste, I believe it will be between a Taylors '27 or a Croft '55.'

'You are so knowledgeable, Harry,' said Rosie, who appeared to be slightly squiffy, 'you're a marvel. You're doing so well.' Wow! I thought. But I suppose to all those present I had, so far, done pretty damn well.

The port decanter was placed on the table next to me, and I charged my glass, carefully tasted it and passed it on to my left. It was definitely one I didn't know well. To ease the tension, since everyone had gone very quiet, I said.

'I thought this might be the easiest as there are very few excellent ports like this one. But before I tell you what I believe it is,' I stood up, 'I'd like to thank Lord Blenkinsopp for providing this wonderful selection of wines, not only for my "trial by wine", but also for us all to enjoy. Will it be four out of four, Auntie B?'

'Whatever happens, Harry, I'm proud of you. I never ever dreamed you would get this far. But I have to admit that I could be out of pocket on this fourth one, as you are a fully paid-up member of the port club from what I can gather,' she said, to roars of friendly laughter round the table.

'Thanks for the compliment, Auntie B. It could of course be that very fine year of 1945, but I surmise that even Lord Blenkinsopp's formidable cellar will have been depleted with countless celebrations to commemorate that year. Then of course it could be a '27, which I believe is when our host was born. How splendid to have been born in such a wonderful year for port. How sad that Tony's birth did not coincide with a vintage year.' Much laughter ensued although there was no hint of a smile on Tony's miserable face. I continued.

'I believe it's either a Croft,' and here I paused for the utmost effect, 'the year being very apt - '55, the year I was born, or, please wait, maybe a Taylors '55. Both very fine vintages. I'm going for the Croft '55. I feel I do know my my ports. I can't imagine why.' I said laughing to ease the tension.

'So it's a Croft '55. Please say I'm right, Lord Blenkinsopp.'

'You are. Well done. Spot on! Congratulations!' he said as everyone got up and came round to shake me by the hand. Sadly I don't remember much more of the evening except that Tony ignored me, and Rosie certainly didn't. And, of course, dear Auntie B made my day by confirming the increase of my allowance by 20%. She said it was something to do with her being a bit tipsy, and a very proud Aunt.

Much later that evening in my room, I asked Reeves, as I drank a whisky nightcap, not caring about my taste buds any more, what young Horace was referring to in the dining room when he said something about me being generous and cleaning my car?

'Well, sir, I happened upon young Horace apparently looking for his mother. I suggested that he tell her his generous Godfather had given him the money for his recent birthday, which I believe you forgot and asked him to clean your car rather than divulge what actually happened.'

'What a cracker, Reeves. Dashed good idea,' I replied. 'Our secret is now safe, I believe. One other thing, Reeves. About the Mini Cooper S.'

Reeves surreptitiously interrupted me, saying,

'Sir, after I heard young Miss Somerset and Miss Rawlings sounding off about how showy and unnecessary Sir Tony Wilmot-Woolley's car was, I hope you don't mind but I took the liberty of cancelling your appointment with Mini Motors on Monday morning. I humbly believe that they will both think that a more grown-up car is more suitable for a man of your calibre and substance. And Sir, I would have to agree with them.'

'Smart of them Reeves, and you. Very smart!'

'And so,' he continued, 'I have arranged for a man to bring a dark green, BMW convertible round to the flat on Monday evening. More your style, Sir, I believe. And the extra 20% will help finance it.'

'More good thinking, Reeves. You really have been using the old grey matter well. Anything else up your sleeve?' I asked as I finished my night-cap.

'Well, there is actually one other small matter, Sir. I took the liberty of booking a table for you and Miss Somerset at The Ivy on Wednesday at eight o'clock. I said you would pick her up in the Strand.'

'Good heavens! You do sometimes work in mysterious ways. Top-hole! Reeves. But why the Strand?' I asked.

'Ah, well Sir. Miss Somerset was so impressed with your

knowledge of wines that she told me she was going to sign up for the next Rothschild lectures, starting on Wednesday.'

'Well done Rosie, old bird! And, Reeves, just one last thing before you go. Take that horrible dinner jacket round to the Red Cross on Monday morning. I always felt it wasn't really me.'

'Thank you Sir. You are quite right of course,' Reeves replied sincerely.

'As usual.'

'If you say so, Sir.'

COLD HEART

They were 'twins' Jeremy Butler and William Shaw, only they were not related, just born on the same day many miles from one another. Neither was to know what great friends they would become. Jeremy's parents lived on a farm in Northumberland, in the middle of nowhere, while William's home was in Chelsea, just off the Embankment. They probably would never have met if it hadn't been for the fact that both their fathers had gone at different times to Ludgrove and then Eton, and had put their boys' names down for both schools at birth.

It was during their first week of their first term at prep school, that they were both introduced to each other.

'Butler, I'd like you to try playing at scrum-half, and you Shaw, fly-half,' old man Brown, the Ludgrove rugger coach suggested, 'I think you'll make a good combination.'

'Hi, Butler,' said William, 'I hate this surname lark. I'm William, okay? And you are?'

'Jeremy. Good to meet you,' and they shook hands.

'Come on you two,' bellowed Brown, 'you'll get to know each other soon enough, once I've taught you the basics. So pay attention, please!'

And that was how they first met. They were to become

inseparable. Jeremy was the shorter of the two, with a stocky build and a shock of jet-black hair. William was taller and better looking, with penetrating dark green eyes, and almost white-blond hair. Their sporting prowess in all games became a legend, and in their last two years the boys played a big part in the school, being undefeated at cricket, rugger and football. Because they were always on the same team there was no rivalry, but squash was altogether a different matter. This was a game at which they were both brilliant. Competitive to the final point, with William always having a slight edge.

'I demand a let,' cried Jeremy, sweating profusely at match point, to him.

'Not on, I'm afraid. You've had your quota. Stop whingeing. You're just ahead, what's the problem?'

'My problem is you always run across me just as I'm about to put away the winning shot. Most unsportsmanlike.'

'I play to win, so please just get on with it. You never know you might manage to beat me one day. Maybe I should play left handed,' William said laughing, and a couple of minutes later he'd won yet again. Mind you, as always, it was very close; 9-7, 8-10, 12-10.

William's height and reach gave him a slight advantage over his friend, and in their five years at Ludgrove, Jeremy had never won a match. Despite this, their friendship continued to flourish, although the headmaster noticed a slight air of superiority in William's manner. But happily this was something that didn't affect the boys' relationship.

At Eton, however, because both fathers had put them down for different houses and they were also in different classes, they didn't see as much of each other as they would have liked. Despite this, the friendship still endured and the squash dog-fights continued.

It was on the playing fields of Eton they had their most fun and success. Both were picked for the 1st XI when just sixteen, and to see Jeremy keeping wicket to William's Warne-like spin bowling was a joy to behold. But however hard he tried, Jeremy could still not work out how to beat his friend at squash.

They both achieved straight 'A' grades in their A levels and, following gap years in Chile and Namibia, were again separated by paternal influences when they went up to Cambridge - Jeremy to Clare College, to read Law, and William to St. John's College, to read Classics.

'Is it true you're seeing Camilla Egerton, that gorgeous, blue stocking from Girton?' William asked, while enjoying crumpets and tea in Jeremy's rooms, halfway through their second term. 'I'm a bit upset actually that I heard about it from another source since I thought you and I had no secrets.'

Jeremy blushed very slightly as he'd never really had any girlfriends before, unlike William who, with his roguish good looks and supreme confidence with women, had had plenty.

'Well-um-er,' he stammered, 'I just thought that for once, this was something I wouldn't share with you straightaway. We've always lived in each other's pockets, which is great up to a point, and they do say two's company and three - well, is a crowd.'

But Jeremy was glad that his secret was out at last and that his old friend had heard it from someone else. He'd kept it from William on purpose, as he could sometimes be a bit over-powering and insensitive. He immediately demonstrated this trait, by asking.

'What's she really like then? She's certainly stunning, but, apparently, as cold as ice. Don't tell me you're going to melt it. Or have you done so already, you sly old bounder!'

For the very first time in their long relationship Jeremy felt his hackles rising slightly, more so when William blundered on.

'Whatever. I am really, really looking forward to meeting her. I might have a pop at her myself if she's proving a bit tricky at you know what. Or perhaps you don't know what?' By now William was laughing mischievously and Jeremy was becoming more and more angry.

'Please William,' he retorted angrily, 'don't be so crude. It's early days and frankly it's none of your business. Let me enjoy myself - without you for a change.'

'I'm sorry. I'm sorry, old chap,' William countered quickly, 'I can see I've hit a very raw nerve. I tell you what, I'll take you both out to dinner in Grantchester tomorrow night, and I'll introduce you to Serena. I think it's Serena I'm seeing this week. I really can't keep track of them. How about it?'

But Jeremy was unhappy - William's attitude to women was "Meet them, bed them and then chuck them". William had never had a girlfriend for more than a few weeks while Jeremy had never really had a girlfriend at all. However he realised that Camilla would have to meet his friend sometime, and so it was agreed that they would get together for dinner in Grantchester.

On the way there the following evening, Camilla was as nervous as Jeremy.

'I really hope I make a good impression for your sake, because I know he's such a great friend. How I just wish I'd worn my denim jacket. I think I look a bit frumpy tonight,' she moaned, but managing to look radiant all the same, and in his eyes far too attractive for the evening ahead. With her stunning looks, long blonde hair and legs up to her armpits, William was bound to be impressed. But not too impressed, Jeremy hoped. Camilla interrupted his thoughts.

'If it's the same William Shaw I've met a couple of times in London, he's gorgeous. And he always has a lovely looking lady by his side. I'm quite surprised I've not met him in Cambridge before. Maybe I'm working too hard. Or maybe it's because you're keeping me happily occupied,' and to prove her point she gave him a tender peck on the cheek.

In the end, William did bring Serena, who was very bubbly and got on well with Jeremy.

'Happy with champagne tonight girls?' William said, summoning a waiter.

'Fine by me,' enthused Camilla.

'Me too,' said Serena, and the party commenced.

Occasionally Jeremy would catch Camilla's eye, and she would give him a reassuring wink. William was certainly paying her a lot of attention. But Jeremy was happy. The atmosphere was good, he did not feel threatened at all and Serena and he had mutual friends from up north, so they had plenty to chat and laugh about.

'So Camilla, what did you think of my charming friend?' Jeremy asked later on their way back to her college.

'Yes, he's certainly a charmer all right! And attractive. But he spent a lot of the evening talking about you. He clearly adores you. And while he's very good company, he's a bit - I'm not sure how to put it - fond of himself. But that happens with those sort of supremely confident guys.'

'Well you looked like you were having lots of fun. Just like old friends.'

'Silly you. Maybe you were just a little jealous? I hope so. But now to a much more important matter. Let's see if this door's still unlocked. Yes! It is. Now I can smuggle you into my rooms and convince you there's only one man in my life and it'll certainly never be William Shaw.'

Naturally a smile spread across Jeremy's face, but at the time he didn't have any idea how those last few words would come back and haunt him.

William and Jeremy didn't see much of each other over the next few days, and it was in the showers, after a game of rugger, that William said;

'I really enjoyed the other evening. Camilla's a great girl. Far too good for you yet intelligent with it. Surely Serena's more your style, perhaps we should swap? No, no, don't worry I'm only kidding. Serena thought you were great, which can't be bad for the old ego.'

Jeremy felt quite chuffed.

'To be honest William I thought you'd either not like Camilla at all, or like her too much. I just wasn't sure.'

'I have to admit to being a bit envious. But you've been my best friend for years and the last thing I would want to do is steal your girlfriend. She probably wouldn't want me anyway. But if things were to go wrong, heaven forbid, I'd like to be the first one to know, so I can pick up the pieces.'

Jeremy felt as though he'd finally got over that hurdle, and they increasingly went out as a foursome, although sadly, Serena was quickly replaced by another, and another, and another, and so it went on. As Jeremy's relationship with Camilla got better and better, he felt far more confident. And all this time the young men's sporting prowess continued, with both of them winning Blues for rugger and cricket, and Half Blues for squash. It became quite a talking point at Cambridge, that while William always beat his friend at squash, Jeremy had what was universally considered to be the ultimate prize - Camilla.

A few years later they both graduated with good Upper Seconds, with Jeremy being articled to a law firm in London and William opting for a career in the City. Naturally they shared a house together, and for that first year they painted the town red. They were inseparable nearly all the time, particularly as Camilla was doing a postgraduate course, and only saw Jeremy occasionally at weekends. Their relationship had continued to blossom but they'd agreed to lead fairly separate lives for a year to see how things panned out. They were still "an item", but free to live their lives as they wished when away from each other.

This suited William well as Jeremy had never lived in London. He was able to introduce him to a lot of his old friends, and take him to a few of his favourite old haunts. Their house was in Chelsea, and nearly every evening they would be out for dinner, and then probably clubbing and a lot more besides. Jeremy had a pink ticket during the academic year. But Camilla was no fool. She knew the score, and decided to tolerate the status quo for the time being. And so it was that Jeremy and William lived life to the full.

They both continued to play cricket, and golf was taken up seriously when they joined Royal Wimbledon Golf Club, where again their rivalry flourished. It would be nice to report that Jeremy always won but that was not the case, although his handicap was lower than his friend's.

Once Camilla had come down from Cambridge, Jeremy's life became rather domesticated, as they had decided to live together in a small house in Battersea. Camilla had a job in the Foreign Office, and the three of them occasionally met for dinner. William invariably brought along yet another new girlfriend, usually some model or budding actress, but very rarely the same girl twice. Once Jeremy questioned William about the length of his relationships.

'I get bored. Can't tell you why. Granted, they're always pretty and willing, but after a while I just get bored and move on. Some people chop and change their cars all the time. I'm like that with women. It's something I'm not proud of. It's just something that happens. It's sad really. All I really want is someone like Camilla. Bright and fun, but caring and loving as well. You're a lucky man. Never forget that. I've often wondered if I'd met her first what would have happened!'

Jeremy didn't bother to answer. William was definitely fishing and he didn't deserve an answer.

And so their lives continued. The two men were still the best of friends, and although Camilla was very much part of their friendship, Jeremy never felt completely relaxed about William's feelings toward her. He knew that William, if given half a chance, would be after her - and it still worried him. It always would. To be fair to Camilla, this was in no way her mind-set, as she became increasingly fed up with William's endless girlfriends that she had to befriend for a while, before they were casually dumped. So it was never a long-lasting, cosy foursome, rather more of a strange threesome, with one member always slightly on his guard - particularly as Camilla was always very friendly towards William.

Once Jeremy had been at Eversheds as a junior partner for a few years he decided he wanted to make his relationship with Camilla more permanent and start a family. He sought his friend's advice over lunch one day.

'Go for it, before she comes knocking at my door. It's okay, I'm only joking. If you don't marry her now some idiot from the Foreign Office will move in, and take her off to somewhere like Madagascar. You can only marry her on two conditions. Firstly, I'm your best man, and secondly, Godfather to your first child.'

'You would have been both anyway,' and Jeremy laughed, 'but not a word to anyone. Tonight's the night, as they say.'

When he got home later that evening he found Camilla in quite a state.

'I need to talk to you darling,' she exclaimed, 'I've got a problem which will affect both our lives.' Jeremy's heart sank.

'Look darling, before you say anything,' and he promptly got down on his knee, and as if on cue, Camilla burst out laughing.

'I don't believe you. I never thought you'd get round to it.'

'Do you mind?' Jeremy said indignantly, 'round to what? Anyway be quiet. Darling Camilla, will you marry me - please?'

'Of course, of course, of course I will. I love you so much. I always have done, ever since I met you at that dreary cocktail party at your college,' whereupon they leapt at each other, ripping everything off as they stumbled into the bedroom for a prolonged engagement ritual.

Later, in the darkness, after some exciting love-making, and between sips of some champagne Jeremy had found hidden away in the kitchen, he asked.

'How selfish can I be? You said you had a problem.'

'Did I? Oh yes. I did, but now thanks to you you've solved it fair and square. You see the Foreign Office was going to send me to Washington, and I really didn't want to leave you. I would have been miserable. But it was that or I was out.'

'So what are you going to do instead? I'm not really sure if I can support the two of us,' Jeremy replied, with a touch of concern in his voice.

Camilla jumped on top of him and said.

'But that's what's so great. Once I'm married I know the Foreign Office will let me stay in London anyway. Although I'm not sure yet what they'll ask me to do, but that'll sort itself out I imagine. My big problem was I didn't want to pressurise you, and now you're going to make me an honest woman for all the right reasons. I'm over the moon. I must ring my parents,' she said picking up the phone.

'Shouldn't I ask your father's permission first?'

'No need. They love you. They'll also be over the moon. I'm so happy,' and she dropped the phone saying, 'come here. My parents can wait! There's some unfinished business to be done. We need to keep practising if we're going to have lots of children.' Jeremy was gently hugged by Camilla, and more practice commenced.

They both agreed that William should be their best man. Before the Stag party Jeremy lost to him, once again, at squash.

'I can't believe that you're actually getting married,' William said later in the bar, 'it's almost as if I'm losing part of my life.'

'Come on. You know Camilla adores you, and you'll always be part of our family,' Jeremy replied.

'Yes, I know. But whilst I've got everything, I still lack a woman like Camilla. Look after her well, because if you don't I will. And that's a promise.'

'So if I keel over you move in. Yes?'

'Yes, and if you treat her badly I would expect her to cry on my shoulder.'

'Fair "dos" I suppose,' Jeremy thought.

The June wedding was a glorious affair. The reception was at Camilla's parents' large estate in Hampshire. The sun shone brightly all day, and William did the decent thing later that night and bedded the maid of honour. So nothing changed.

Inevitably, after the wedding, Jeremy and William began to see less of each other. Camilla juggled her life between being a mother and a senior manager at the Foreign Office while her nanny strived to look after their two children, who only had a year between them in age, and were both quite a handful. As promised, William was Godfather to their elder boy, George, and would occasionally appear for Sunday lunch with his latest conquest and a generous present for his Godson.

And so the years went by, the happy couple's children grew up, while William didn't settle down, and Jeremy always lost at squash.

'Do you think you'll ever get married William?' Jeremy asked him after a squash match where he'd suffered yet another defeat.

'I doubt it. I just can't seem to find what you have. Camilla is the perfect wife and mother. I'm very envious of you. You would have thought that by now, with all the women I've shacked up with over the years, one would prove a winner. But I set high standards, and the highest standard will always be your wife. I've always adored her and yet I love you as my greatest friend. It's just sad you won and I didn't.'

'You say that. But if you'd met Camilla first and maybe

if I hadn't been around, how are you so certain she would have fallen for you?' Jeremy asked quizically.

'Simple. You and I have always been the greatest of friends from way back. That's the common link. We're too similar for Camilla not to have fallen for me.' Indeed Camilla and William did always seem to get on very well, which still occasionally worried Jeremy.

While both their lives were unfolding with Jeremy became one of the senior partners at Eversheds, William, however, was destined for greater things. Politics called, and once elected as an MP he soon became a Junior Minister, and then Minister of Sport. As a public figure the nature of the friends' relationship changed, due to William's many public engagements. Security was tight, and it meant that although Jeremy had been vetted, they had less occasion to meet, although William did try and make Sunday lunch at least once a month and play the occasional game of squash, and very occasionally, golf.

William was a member of the new House of Commons Health Club, which was situated in Victoria, and housed an excellent gym, sauna and steam room, as well as three squash courts. Again security was tight, as it was only used by Members of Parliament and their very close friends. The last time Jeremy played there he was amused to see that William secreted a Thermos flask of dry martini into the steam room. Drink was strictly banned from any area in the club, except for the small bar. He'd also noticed that, stripped down, his friend had put on a lot of weight, and the last time he'd come for Sunday lunch, he'd drunk three dry martinis before lunch followed by more than a bottle of claret with the roast beef.

Next time he saw William for a drink, he broached the

subject.

'It's not a problem. Ministers are under a lot of stress. Yes, we drink a lot but we work bloody hard. It's okay for you, you've got the lovely Camilla to keep you on the straight and narrow. My love life is in tatters. I have to be seen with the right type of people. Sleaze is endemic, and very young girls are not good for my image. If you must know, but keep it quiet, I've been celibate for quite awhile. I can't risk the young ones and women of my age are married, divorced or, if still single, desperate. Whichever it is, they now tend to steer clear of me, unimpressed by my track record. So all in all, I'm a pretty tragic figure. How do you feel now?' he said as he ordered his third dry martini. 'What are you going to have?'

'Nothing thanks. I've got to drive back to Wimbledon. I feel sorry for you, but what can I do?'

Angry and drunk William suddenly turned on Jeremy, and said in a loud voice.

'Why don't you just drop dead, and I can then marry Camilla. She's the one I need now and she's always been far too good for you. I'm sorry, I really am. I shouldn't have said that but you have such a lovely family life and although I'm seen as successful Minister, I'd trade all that for what you have.'

'What you should do,' Jeremy retorted loudly, 'is lay off the juice!'

'Don't you start pontificating! You're always happy to have an illicit martini in the steam room, so don't be such a hypocrite. Just leave me alone.'

And that was that. For the time being.

It was the following day, at work, that Bill Evans hit Jeremy with the bombshell. He was the Senior Partner and one of Jeremy's favourite colleagues at Eversheds. He'd approached him in the corridor and said;

'I need a private word with you. I'll see you in your office at 3.30 pm.'

He'd seemed agitated, and as it was only just after lunch, Jeremy had plenty of time for conjecture. Business had been difficult recently and the firm had laid off staff and generally cut back. However, Jeremy's department had been flourishing, and if anything was probably the biggest earner in the partnership. The time went by very slowly, as Jeremy racked his brains as to what it might be about. There was a knock on his door at precisely 3.30 pm.

'Come on in Bill. I know it's you. You're never ever late for any meeting. One could set a clock by you. Pull up a chair and let me know what's on your mind.'

'Thanks Jeremy. This is not going to be easy, and I hope I'm not sticking my neck out too far. How long has your wife known William Shaw?

'What a strange question. They met at Cambridge, surely you knew that? Is there a problem?' Jeremy replied anxiously.

'Well it may be nothing at all, but over the last few weeks I've seen your wife lunching with William, more than once, and always deep in conversation. Also, I was at that Foreign Office "do" you couldn't make the other day, and he spent the whole evening talking to her. It's a well known fact that you three are good friends, but it was just the intensity of their conversation that made me feel I had to let you know what I'd seen. I hope I've done the right thing. You've always been such a good friend.'

'Well to be honest they've known each other for years. But thanks for telling me, and please don't worry too much about it. I certainly won't.'

Bill rose to leave, shook Jeremy by the hand and was clearly happy to have got it off his chest. Jeremy followed him to the door, shut and locked it.

He paced up and down his office. At the back of his mind he'd always worried something like this might happen. And he had noticed, over the last couple of months, how much more friendly Camilla had been towards William. Their body language indicated that there was some sort of secret between them, but still Jeremy couldn't bring himself to believe that they were having an affair. Camilla had recently been decidedly off-hand and edgy, which was very unlike her. When Jeremy mentioned it to her she was quite short with him, although she did apologise later saying she was very busy at work.

Jeremy agonised. Should he confront her or was he over-reacting? The fact that Bill Evans (good old reliable, trustworthy Bill), of all people, had told him made him feel that there could well be something going on under his very nose. He felt both helpless and confused but above all, let down. Just then his phone rang and his thoughts were unhappily confirmed.

'Hello darling, it's me,' Camilla said sounding very cheerful, 'I hope you don't mind, but William has got a spare seat for the opera tonight, and has asked me to go to Madam Butterfly at the Royal Opera House. You don't mind do you? We'll probably go on somewhere for dinner, so don't wait up as I'll probably be home quite late.'

'Fine. You go out and have a good time. I've got quite a lot of work to catch up on.'

'You sound upset. I won't go if you don't want me to,' she replied unconvincingly.

'No. No. Please. Have a good time. I'm busy right now. Bye.'

Jeremy refrained from slamming down the phone. His gravest doubts seemed to be materialising. Over the past years she'd often gone to the opera with William as Jeremy wasn't that keen, but she always came straight home afterwards. He sat down and thought about their marriage. Was it going wrong? They weren't as intimate as before but he felt this was a function of age, rather than a lack of love. Maybe it wasn't, maybe she was having an affair with William. She'd certainly been a bit off recently. But for the moment he felt he must give her the benefit of the doubt.

In the middle of the following week Camilla worked late two evenings running, something she very rarely did, and William also cancelled their usual squash match on one of those evenings. Jeremy had no one to turn to. He felt he was being betrayed by his two best friends. He made up his mind. He had to talk to her. He was about to pick up the phone to fix up lunch that day with Camilla, when it rang. It was his son George, who he adored.

'Hi Dad. Have you got a minute?' he asked sounding worried.

'Yes, of course. Fire away. Are you okay?' Jeremy replied.

'I'm fine Dad, I think.'

What George told his father was not good news. On one of the evenings Camilla had worked late, George and some of his friends had been in a cocktail bar in Covent Garden. He'd seen his mother deep in conversation with his Godfather, and when she looked up she looked straight through him, as though she didn't even recognise her own son.

'Dad, I'm concerned. Is everything okay with you and Mum?'

'Yes, of course. Everything's fine,' Jeremy lied, 'she's probably helping him refurbish his new flat in Westminster, or something like that. So don't worry. I'll sort it out with your Mum.'

'Thanks Dad. Sorry to have bothered you, but it upset me a bit, and I thought you ought to know.'

So she didn't acknowledge her own son. Jeremy's blood boiled. He again locked his door, sank down behind his desk and pummelled his forehead. He had already confronted his wife a few weeks ago about William. They'd had a huge row, and she'd stormed out, calling him a silly man and a sadly jealous husband who should just try and grow up.

What a bastard, he thought! And actually, what a bitch! But a bitch or not he didn't want to lose her to William. That would be totally unbearable. Suddenly the whole scenario just hit him where it really hurt, and he felt physically sick and mentally drained. Drastic action was needed. Jeremy was not prepared to lose his wonderful wife to his best friend, or someone he had always thought was his best friend. Events had now convinced Jeremy that they must have been having an affair for a while. The evidence was there, and had become more noticeable now that he thought about it. He just couldn't bear to think of William and his wife being together, whatever the circumstances. He could not carry on his life any longer knowing that they were seeing each other. How far had they gone? The thought filled him with revulsion. He must act, and act fast, before his marriage fell apart. He wanted William out of the way forever and as soon as possible. And that meant, dead.

But how? He racked his brains for some time, and then, suddenly, looking out of his window, he had the answer. London had been in the grip of the coldest February for years and there was his answer - icicles. That was it. It all clicked into place. Many years ago, as a child, he'd read a story about a man who was murdered when a sharp icicle was plunged into his heart. It took place in a steam room, and the one thing he particularly remembered was that it hardly left any mark at all. The murder weapon was obviously never found, and the murderer got away scot-free. It was a heaven-sent opportunity for Jeremy. He was due to play squash against William the following evening, if it wasn't cancelled, and it was his turn to mix the martinis. Whilst security was tight at the club, all the guards knew their unusual habit of always taking in a Thermos flask of dry martini, so that would not prove a problem. All he now had to do was select an appropriate icicle, sharpen it and put the murder weapon into the flask. What could be simpler?

Jeremy knew he had to leave work early to find the said "weapon". The freeze was more severe out in Wimbledon where he lived, and he was convinced he'd find a suitable icicle there. Later, walking outside around the house, he was spoilt for choice and selected four large icicles which he placed inside a large Thermos flask he was carrying and then went to his workshop where he chiselled them down into sharp daggers no more than about six inches long, so that the best one would fit snugly into William's dry martini Thermos flask. With the job done to his satisfaction he left them at the back of the deep-freeze.

Just then the phone in his workshop rang.

'Are you all right darling? I rang your office and they said you'd gone home early feeling shivery.'

'Oh, I'm okay. I feel a bit fluey so I'll probably take tomorrow off,' Jeremy replied.

'I actually phoned to let you know I'll be home a bit late,

as I've got to see William for a drink at his new flat.'

Jeremy controlled his rage, and replied through clenched teeth.

'Why on earth are you seeing him there?'

But there was no reply as she rang off.

Now Jeremy was more convinced than ever. He phoned the office at 5.30pm to say he really wasn't feeling too good, and wouldn't make it in the next day. He then phoned William's office and just caught him before he left. They arranged to meet at their usual time the following day and then Jeremy casually asked,

'Up to anything exciting this evening?'

'No, actually I'm going to what could be a rather dull art gallery reception in St. James. You've got my Thermos as it's your turn to mix the martinis, isn't it? Make them strong. See you tomorrow.'

If you're going to have an affair, at least be consistent with your story, Jeremy thought, fuming. He barely spoke to his wife on her return, as she was late and far too happy for his liking.

'Take tomorrow off darling,' she said as she got ready for bed, 'hopefully you'll feel well enough for your game of squash with William in the evening.'

'I'm sure I will,' Jeremy countered angrily as he turned his light off.

The next day was like a bad dream for Jeremy. Once Camilla had left for work he just lay there remembering all the good times he'd had with William, and how on numerous occasions William had remarked how much Camilla meant to him. Well sod him, he thought, now all that's finished.

Jeremy decided, after a leisurely breakfast, to play some

golf in the freezing cold to clear his head. The Pro at Royal Wimbledon agreed to join him, and they had an excellent game, Jeremy just winning at the last.

Once he got home, he carefully chose his weapon from the icicles he'd placed in the deep freeze the night before, melting down the other three. Later he made his way, by taxi, to the House of Commons club. Security proved no problem.

'Your usual tipple I see Mr. Butler. I'm sure the Minister will be pleased about that. Don't worry, that Thermos flask doesn't have to go through the X-ray machine. It might shake the martini up too much,' the guard said laughing.

During the match Jeremy's adrenalin was pumping through his body so fast that he actually beat William for the very first time in his life.

'I just can't believe it. You've actually won at last!' said William incredulously. 'You've beaten me. You've never ever beaten me. What's got into you? Camilla said you've been a bit down recently but why take it out on me? The dry martini had better be very, very dry because I'm most upset. Our squash games go back over forty years at least, and you've never, ever beaten me. Why this evening?'

The victory was in a way bittersweet for Jeremy, but with a pleasant irony to it. After stripping off both men went into the steam room, Jeremy clasping the Thermos and two glasses close to his chest. The room was actually quite large with a couple of people, hardly visible, sitting in a corner.

'Come on old chap, this time I really do need my martini more than ever. I still can't believe you actually beat me,' William said.

As William peered through the steam at the other people in the room, Jeremy coolly undid the Thermos, took out the sharp icicle, tapped his friend on the shoulder, and as he turned, chose his spot carefully and plunged the icicle straight between William's ribs straight into his heart. He pushed hard until the icicle disappeared completely. William exhaled violently, slumped back against the wall and sat there looking as though he had just dozed off. There was a tiny speck of blood which Jeremy duly wiped away with a rather damp tissue, which he later flushed down the loo.

Jeremy got up quickly, and went into the showers, hoping that no one would discover William straightaway. However it seemed only a few minutes later, that one of the stewards told him William had been found dead in the steam room. No one should leave the club, as the police would be arriving shortly.

'They think it was probably a stroke. I'm sorry sir. I know how close you both were,' the steward remarked.

'Thank you Jack. This is an awful shock. If I'm needed, I'll be in the bar. He seemed fine when I left for my shower.'

It was likely that the law would find no motive or any sign of the murder weapon. Jeremy had probably committed the perfect murder.

After being questioned by the police he was allowed to leave the club. The general consensus was that William had had a massive cardiac arrest, brought on by stress and over exertion on the squash court. It had been rumoured that William's drink problem was quite severe, and that he'd steadily been putting on weight. So it was felt by the police that, prior to a post-mortem being carried out, all these factors had probably contributed to his untimely death.

In the cab on the way home, Jeremy phoned his wife. She had seen the news on Sky TV and was in a terrible state.

As soon as he was through the front door, Camilla ran out of the sitting-room to meet him and wept hysterically on his shoulder. After a while she calmed down, and as they walked back into the drawing-room she asked him quietly, in a controlled voice:

'Darling how awful for you! Tell me, what happened?'

'There's not really a lot to say. One minute he was very much alive and then I heard he'd suffered what they think was a cardiac arrest, while still in the steam room. Look Camilla, I know this isn't the right time, but I desperately need an answer from you. Had you been seeing William on the quiet? Please tell me. Were you having an affair? Was it serious? How long has it been going on for? You must tell me. I need to know. Now!' he said, his voice choking.

'Darling, darling Jeremy. I can state, quite categorically, that I was not having, and never have had, an affair with William. What on earth's got into you? Although, of course, I have been seeing quite a lot of him over the last few weeks.'

'Yes I know all that. My friends and George have kept me well informed. What on earth's been going on? Please tell me before I go completely mad!' he said shouting at his wife.

'For goodness sake Jeremy, please don't be so emotional. I know you're upset, but you're being over-dramatic. Pour us a drink. We both need one and I'll explain everything.'

Jeremy, shaking badly, poured out two large, neat whiskies and sat opposite his wife and pleaded, 'Surprise me, please!'

'Are you sure you're okay now? Because there is a very simple explanation,' she said slowly, looking her husband straight in the eye. 'All William and I have been doing was planning a secret joint birthday party in April for your fiftieth and George's twenty-fifth. If you suspected we were having an affair, then yes, you are not just mad, but mental. And talking of being mental, can you explain why, when I came home last night and was looking for some ice for my whisky nightcap, I found at least four sharply pointed icicles hidden away, right at the back of the deep-freeze? They looked dangerous, more like stiletto knives and could have done someone some serious damage. Why on earth were they there anyway? Oh, my God! - you didn't…?!'

ECONOMICAL WITH THE TRUTH

Life had been pretty tough on Eddie Johnson and his family. Eddie was a barrister in his late fifties who, up until the last couple of years, had enjoyed a pretty successful career. He'd seen both his children through public school, and they were now honing both their academic and non-academic skills (such as binge drinking) at university and generally having a good time. Money had not been a problem, which meant two good holidays a year away with the children, and a couple of short breaks with his wife of twenty-five years, Carole.

"Thank God for Carole," he thought, cutting the grass late one September evening, "I could never have coped without her."

She had supplemented the family income by becoming a very successful travel writer, which should have surprised no one, as she had a very high profile career in journalism when they were first married. When Eddie told the family he was getting fewer and fewer briefs, Carole had already worked out a plan of action, which she announced to her family one day over Sunday lunch.

'You needn't worry. It's certainly not your fault, darling. It's the Chambers and your clerks. I am sure they feel you've had your just desserts, and they are giving the work to your younger colleagues who are moving up the ladder. Actually, as a family we needn't worry because I'll be the breadwinner soon as I've been commissioned to write a book.'

'You write a book! What sort of a book?' asked Jack, their twenty-year-old son who was waiting to go back up to Durham university.

'A book that you, Harriet and your age group will enjoy.'

'Something we'll both enjoy! Unlikely!' said Harriet, 'we're like chalk and cheese, you know that.' Harriet was in her last year at Cambridge reading PPE and didn't rate Durham that highly.

'I know you are very different. I accept that. But there is one thing you both enjoy and enjoy doing together. Right?'

'Skiing?' they both asked.

'Yes, skiing. I'm going to write a guidebook on popular European ski resorts such as Val d'Isère, Meribel, Tignes Courchevel and a few others.'

'So what's going to be so different from all the other guidebooks on Val d'Isère, Tignes, Courchevel, etc etc?' asked Eddie.

'Good question. It will be aimed at the young, specifically those children with very little money, who have just left university and are no longer getting their holidays paid for by their parents - people who are dedicated skiers in the day and party hard at night. Let's face it, over the years I've been to all the top ski resorts. And remember, I was a chalet girl for two seasons, and your father a plongeur, something he'd rather forget,' she added, laughing.

The Johnson family were fanatical skiers. The parents had met in Val d'Isère and both the children had done Ski le Gap in Canada. Most years they took two skiing holidays, and as Carole mentioned, had been to all the top Swiss, Austrian, French and Italian ski resorts.

'You've kept this very quiet,' said her husband, 'I was getting a little bit worried about all the trips to London you've been making these last couple of months.'

'Actually I really wanted to let you all know what I've been up to, and the deal I've negotiated. And for once, we're all together, which doesn't happen very often, so I can now tell you, "en famille", as it were.'

'What's the deal?' asked her husband.

'It's the deal I've made with my old boss Jim Freeman at the Daily Telegraph, who's now their main travel editor. You remember him don't you darling?'

'Who wouldn't? Pompous and brash.'

'That's as maybe. His paper has decided to underwrite my research costs, publish the book and feature it as one of their special offers.'

'Well done, Mum,' Harriet enthused, 'I suppose that means revisiting the resorts; you lucky thing.'

'Yes, it certainly does. I hope you don't mind,' she said to Eddie, 'but I'll be away next year for three months, January to March. The good news about the deal is that we all, as a family, get a week's free skiing in Courchevel which is my final destination. Jim Freeman and his family will be joining us there.'

And so come January, Carole, went about her task. Her only brief was to stay in small family-run hotels or tour operators' chalets, so people could tailor-make their holiday. These inexpensive hotels were ideal for Carole to build weekend breaks around, whereas the chalets catered for parties a week at a time. Over those three months, she visited

Lech, Klosters, Zermatt, Davos, Chamonix, Tignes, Val d'Isère, Meribel among others and, finally Courchevel. None of them were at all similar, although national characteristics were very apparent. She had had a wonderful time, but was looking forward to her family finally arriving at the resort..

Jim Freeman had phoned Eddie and arranged to meet him in the departure area at Gatwick Airport. As neither of them could remember what the other looked like, Jim said he would be wearing a red rose in his buttonhole.

'Nothing out of the ordinary for me, old chap,' he had said to Eddie on the phone the previous week when the arrangements were being made.

'I often wear a rose in my lapel. Any old colour, but probably red, don't you know?'

Eddie certainly did not know, but was beginning to remember that on the few occasions he had met Jim he'd found him an insufferable bore.

He shared his concern with the children on the way to Gatwick.

'Don't worry Dad,' said Harriet, 'I'm sure we won't see that much of them.'

However that was not to be the case, certainly as far as Eddie was concerned. He was right to be worried when he saw Jim, who he vaguely remembered. Looking larger than life, Jim was accompanied by his family presumably, and was wearing a startlingly large yellow, not red, rose. Jim could hardly have missed him.

'Hi Jim. I'm Eddie and this is Harriet and Jack.'

'Splendid. Wonderful to meet you all,' Jim boomed, resulting in raised eyebrows from both Eddie's children, as Jim pumped Eddie's outstretched hand.

'Now then Eddie, this is my wife Sylvia and the children,

Mark and Helen.' Eddie took one look at Sylvia and two words came to mind - "down trodden".

'Pleased to meet you, I'm sure, Eddie,' she twittered.

'Wonderful woman my wife. Does everything I ask and more, don't you darling?' Jim shouted to his wife and all their fellow travellers, queuing at Gate H. Eddie soon realised that he was going to be left at the mercy of this very loud person. The children, it appeared, had mutual friends at various schools and universities and were happily chatting away.

'Now then, Eddie, tell me about yourself. Your darling lady wife told me your briefs had dried up, what?' he said laughing uncontrollably. 'A joke, old chap. Don't look so forlorn. I'd better sit next to you on the flight and we'll have a few drinks to cheer you up.'

Eddie knew when he was beaten and sat throughout the entire flight being told by Eddie what a wonderful skier he was. He had only taken it up recently but was a natural. You know the sort don't you, dear reader? Steer well clear or they bend your ear. Eddie sat bemused as this man regaled him with far-fetched skiing yarns. Far-fetched as he had only been skiing three or four times - ever.

"We'll soon see", thought Eddie. "The proof of the pudding and all that". He did, however, manage to interrupt him with one quick question.

'Why the yellow rose and not the red one as we agreed?'

'Red was it? All the same to me. Sorry, I often mix my colours up.'

Still, Jim did have his uses, because on arrival at Lyon airport, a minibus was waiting to whisk them off to Courchevel.

Carole had booked them all into The Hotel, which was

fairly basic and inexpensive, which was what her book was all about.

'See you all for a noggin before dinner,' Jim boomed as he went upstairs to his room. Shortly afterwards Jack and Harriet joined their parents in their room.

'Wow!' said Jack, 'that Jim is way too over-the-top. Even his own children said they found him embarrassing, and have asked to ski with Harriet and me! Not with their parents.'

'So, it's down to you, Mum and Dad to look after him. After all, Mum, he's sort of your boss.'

'Yes, you're right I suppose. Dad said he didn't draw breath on the plane and just meeting him now for a few minutes, he seems to be into overdrive. Maybe he'll settle down.'

'I doubt it' said Eddie softly, 'anyway we can at least be just us, "en famille", for dinner.'

'I'm afraid not, darling,' Carole said, 'there are no tables for four in the hotel's dining room, just eight or twelve. We'll have to sit with them.'

'Give me strength,' moaned Eddie as Jack offered him a glass of whisky, saying 'I think you're going to need this.'

'It's only for a week Dad, and it's important for Mum to be civil isn't it?' Harriet said.

'Within reason, yes,' her mother replied. 'The contract to publish is already signed although I've not finished writing the book, so please be patient, darling.'

'I will, I will,' said Eddie sulkily, swigging his glass of whisky. 'I'm going to need a few more of these before the week is out, otherwise I might do that buffoon an injury.'

'Many a true word spoken in jest, darling,' Carole remarked, 'but please try to be civil to him.'

But things went from bad to worse. Dinner was a nightmare. They did all have to share a table and whilst the children were all getting along well with one another, Jim ensured the adults were not.

'What's this dreadful wine they've given us? I don't remember ordering it,' he said in a voice loud enough to have everyone in the room listening .

'No, Jim, that's the way it is and I'm afraid there's no choice. The same with the food. It's why I am here doing my book. Can't you understand? I did warn you that we would be holidaying here on the cheap. This is the sort of place I've been researching for the last three months.'

'Well, I think it's preposterous. The wine is undrinkable and the food not much better.'

And so it went on and on throughout dinner. That was the bad bit, but the worst occurred the following morning when Sylvia did not come down to breakfast.

'Bloody place has given the poor old thing food poisoning. Of course I've got a stomach like an ox but really, it's not on. Still Carole and Eddie, you can have the pleasure of my company today if you don't mind. I've not skied here before so I'll tag along with you two. Should be great fun, what! Shan't miss the old gal a bit. ("Oh yes you will", thought Eddie) So what's the plan? Straight to the top, that's always my motto at ski resorts. No point in mucking about with all those beginners on the lower slopes, don't you agree, Eddie?'

'Yes, if you're up for it.'

'Of course I am. I'm not some lily-livered old Englishman. I've been looking at the resort map with all the runs on and they all look pretty straightforward, don't you know?'

Just then Carole walked over and said, 'I suggest, Jim, we

stop halfway up the mountain, and do a couple of runs to get our acts together. Then we tackle the higher stuff later in the morning.'

'Nonsense, woman, I'm perfectly capable of taking on any run. I like to make my own way down, so all you need to do is point me in the right direction and I'll be off.'

"Suits me," thought Eddie.

Conditions that morning were really excellent, with clear blue skies. The pistes had been "groomed" and looked like icing sugar on a wedding cake. Because of Jim's supreme confidence, Carole and Eddie relented and agreed to go right to the top of the mountain.

'I hear your two have agreed to ski with Mark and Helen. Damn decent of them, what?'

The view from halfway up the mountain was breathtaking and even Jim was quiet for a while. As they all trooped out off towards the next cable car, Jim remarked.

'Just can't believe the amount of dreadful people there are around and, now, dammit, we're going to have to queue again. What a pain!'

'Well it is Easter. You'll find most of the lifts will be very crowded.' said Carole, beginning to sound slightly exasperated.

'Can't be helped, eh? Let's push our way through these bods and get onto the next cable car. I hate waiting around,' said Jim - who else?

'You are very quiet this morning, Eddie,' observed Carole, whispering into her husband's ear.

'Not really, just thinking,' he replied.

'Always worrying, darling. Anyway, cheer up. The skiing is going to be great and I'm sure Jim will improve.'

'I doubt it somehow.'

'When we get to the top,' Jim interrupted loudly, 'if the main run is very crowded, Eddie, could you please point me in the direction of one that is likely to have less plebs on it on it. Not a black run though at this stage, don't you know?'

'I certainly will,' Eddie replied, smiling.

'Come on everybody,' Jim shouted, as the cable car began emptying, 'get a move on.'

Once they were out at the top, there were inevitably a lot of people around.

'There are far too many skiers up here. I'm ready to go but not with that bloody shower, what? I wonder why nobody's doing this blue run over here?' he said squinting into the sunlight. 'It looks blue to me and it says it's open. I'm going to give it a go. See you later.'

'Have fun, Jim,' said Eddie as he watched Jim peeling off to the right and disappearing down the steep slope.

Carole, meanwhile, had met a friend on the cable car and therefore had missed Eddie's conversation with Jim.

'Where's Jim, darling?'

'He insisted on doing that run over there as no one else was doing it.'

'What! Hardly surprising, you fool! That's a black run and it's probably the most difficult one in the resort! It's clearly a black run, for God's sake. Didn't you know he's been suffering from an extremely rare form of colour blindness? Surely he told you?'

'No,' Eddie replied truthfully, 'he never actually told me - in so many words.'

ABSOLUTE FOLLY

Toby had had a bad day. The meeting he had attended near Oxford was not a success. He worked in IT and had been trying to sell to potential clients the idea of their large business centre being totally re-networked for greater speed. It had been a bit like talking to a brick wall. Progress did not seem to be on the agenda that day, although it was they who had originally made contact with his firm, Technophile.

Still, if he pushed on a bit, he should make his local in Wandsworth by six thirty, if the traffic wasn't too bad. But then he decided to go back via Henley-on-Thames, where his grandparents had lived, for old times sake, which might delay him a bit.

Toby Jones was a successful young businessman in his late twenties, with blue eyes and close cropped fair hair, tall, rangy and interesting looking rather than classically so. He had a strong personality, and was never short of friends, although a four year relationship had recently ended amicably. He still yearned for companionship but was not about to fall in love again too quickly. Freedom was good and he was beginning to enjoy it.

As he bombed down the A4130 between Nettlebed and Henley, at around 90 miles an hour in his brand new

Porsche convertible, life seemed almost bearable. Until - BANG! the car veered out of control across the road, with Toby desperately swerving to the left to compensate, and braking hard.

'S**t!' he shouted out loud. 'I must have had a bloody blow-out,' as he steered the car into a convenient lay-by.

'F**k! F**k! F**k!' he exclaimed, remembering he had left his AA card at home in his rush to get out that morning. The car was only a week old, and he hadn't really listened to the salesman when he ran through a few simple things that might happen, like the roof jamming or more relevantly, changing a wheel. Toby vaguely remembered him saying that each alloy wheel was worth over £750, which was why one of the bolts on each wheel had a locking system. He found the Porsche manual, and looked up the tyre section. Being useless mechanically, but having exemplary DIY skills, he thought he might be able to cope by looking at this dilemma from a DIY perspective. Having read the appropriate section which explained in simple Germanic detail what needed to be done, Toby set about the task. He located the tool kit under the bonnet, complete with jack and wheel brace.

"So far so good," he thought, as he found the jack point just under the driver's door. He placed the jack in the allotted place and began to take some of the load off the wheels. This was not made any easier as it was a fairly narrow lay-by, and it felt as though the passing traffic was brushing his backside. Still it was a fine afternoon, and Toby realised once he had found the key, that it should not take him long to be back on the road. He thought the key would be in the tool box - it wasn't. He then vaguely remembered that the car salesman had mentioned a specific place it was kept for safety reasons, as it could easily fall out of the toolbox.

'Toby! You idiot! Where is it?' he shouted above the roar of the traffic. He felt a fool, but he had a good brain, and by a process of elimination he plumped for the glove compartment, having already looked in the ashtray and the back pocket of the manual. And there it was, fixed magnetically to the top of the glove compartment in true Teutonic style.

"Yes! Yes! Yes!" he chortled happily, as he took his newly-found trophy round to the puncture. He located the rogue nut with the lock and tried to unlock it. Nothing happened, the key just went round and round like a front door key when the barrel won't take.

'Oh S**t! I don't believe it,' and as he said this an identical Porsche pulled up behind him and out stepped a stunningly attractive woman.

Maggie Webb, had coincidentally, also been at a meeting near Oxford, and was driving herself home to Chelsea in her convertible Porsche, when she drove past Toby. She had noticed his car and a poor guy trying to change his wheel. As she wasn't in much of a hurry, (the au pair was looking after the children, and her husband, Neil, an accountant in the City, had been lunching somewhere), she decided to turn around and offer to help.

Nothing ventured, nothing gained, and one ought really to stick by one's fellow Porsche owners, she mused.

'Hi! You look as if you might need some help,' she said smiling as she got out of her car. He looked fit, she thought, and was glad she had turned round and come back.

'Thanks. I do. It looks like the lock is malfunctioning as the barrel just goes round and round,' he replied feeling rather helpless, but looking more interesting by the minute to Maggie. Toby also had the same vibes and although she was probably at least fifteen years older than he was, she looked very attractive, with a slim figure and long legs highlighted by a well-cut suit. More leg was shown, to his delight, as she bent down to take a closer look.

'One thing my father taught me when I first learnt to drive was how to change a wheel. Sorting the oil and water are just common sense. Whenever I get a new car I always check the manual on how to change the wheel. To be honest, now I always ring the AA, and sit in my locked car until they arrive. Having said that, you might wonder why I am here? Let's just put it down to fellow Porsche owners - for the moment!' she said smiling broadly at Toby who was, for once, lost for words.

'Let me have the key,' Maggie continued, 'don't feel useless, as they are not easy to unlock. You need to twiddle the key around a bit in the lock until it clicks. Yes, done it! Now the bolt will ease off and you can change the tyre. It's just a knack. I had a flat tyre at our cottage the other weekend, and I decided to change the tyre myself to keep my hand in, and I admit it took a while for me to master the lock. So voilà I've done it. It's all yours.'

As she got up, Simon realised again what a beautiful woman she was and said.

'I really can't thank you enough. I suppose you are my fairy godmother in a Versace suit.'

'Chanel actually,' she said smiling and they both laughed.

'I hope you can manage now. I see yours is the latest model. You must run a successful business.'

'I'm in IT, which at the moment is paying well, and this is my company car. Please take my business card. You never know, it might be of use to you one day.'

Well, it might, she thought. But not on the business front. She had something very different in mind. She did not give him her card as that might appear too forward, but she had his, and that was all that mattered.

'Well, Toby,' she said, looking at his the card, 'nice meeting you. I'll be in touch if I need you.'

'Fine and thanks again, er...' he paused, obviously wanting her name.

'It's Maggie Webb, Toby. Ciao.' She shook his hand, turned and walked back to her car.

What a lady, he thought as she climbed in and moved out into the traffic, hooted and waved goodbye. If only she had been a bit younger. Somehow she reminded him a bit of Mrs Robinson in The Graduate - partly because he had felt nervous and out of control in her company. He had always gone out with girls younger than himself, and he was invariably the dominant partner. But Maggie was something else. Married with two kids, he conjectured, as he changed the wheel, and with a loving husband who was "something in the City".

He thought about her a lot on his way back to London but, once he got to The Ship, in Wandsworth and met his friends, she was soon forgotten.

However, he could not have been more wide of the mark concerning Maggie or her husband. She was the major breadwinner. Having graduated from Oxford with a First in Classics, she joined a top firm of lawyers, and was now at forty-two a senior partner, specialising in International Law with a particular responsibility for European Law, which meant she travelled extensively. She was highly successful whilst her husband, Neil, struggled in the City. The only reason they had ever been able to afford any holidays was through the many Air Miles she clocked up each year. Maggie loved Neil, but did not really respect him. He was too nice in business and had never really made the grade. But they were, on the whole, a happy family with two lovely children, dog, cat, country cottage and lots of good friends. So Maggie was content with her lot rather than sublimely happy. She believed she was probably nearing a mid-life crisis. Her sex life was good but predictable, as it often is when you know your way round your partner's body like the back of your hand. Many of her girlfriends felt the same, but family life was special and so they all carried on with the accepted status quo. She had had a few one-night stands whilst away on business, but that was more self-gratification than anything else.

Strangely she had thought no more about her encounter with Toby, although at the time, she had experienced a certain something. She filed his card under I for IT and just wished she was younger. Who knows what might have happened?

Likewise, Toby got on with his work and social whirl and only occasionally remembered his meeting with Maggie. After a few weeks he thought no more about it. That was until he received a text message from her that made him think about her again and what an impression she had made.

At her practice Maggie was a stickler for punctuality and tidiness. Tidiness meant more than just keeping her office tidy. It meant everything was immaculately filed. This included her rather ancient card index file which she religiously went through every three months, as in her line of business she was forever meeting new people and picking up the inevitable business cards. To do this, she stayed late one evening and eventually she came to I for IT, and there was Toby's card. As she held it in her hand it somehow warmed her fingers as if it was saying something. She sat there at her desk fondly remembering their brief encounter, and wondered whether he still remembered her. She could even recall what she was wearing and how he had struck her in a deeply physical way. She suddenly realised she was shaking, and there was a warm glow in her stomach. She had to contact him and get some sort of dialogue going without committing either of them. She thought it could be fun to instigate a sort of electronic romance, and if anything came of it, so be it. She always loved it when her mobile beeped and displayed an icon advising that a new message had been received, as it was never business and normally from her children at school or one of her girlfriends. So what to say? Something, maybe a bit risqué and romantic, to see how he responded. There was certainly nothing to lose and she realised if they struck up a text relationship, it could be rather enjoyable.

At the other side of town, Toby was drinking in a bar in Battersea with a girl called Sophie, who he had just met at a party that weekend. They were sussing each other out, which was proving great fun, and they seemed to be getting along famously. Sophie was the first girl he had met in weeks who came anywhere close to his last girlfriend.

'Please turn your mobile off when you are flirting with me,' Sophie said laughing.

'Are you sure it's mine, I felt no vibration.'

'I'll provide those if you're lucky,' she retorted cheekily, which he loved.

'It's only a text. I'll read it later.'

'No, go on. I'm inquisitive. Texts can be such fun and I

want to see how amusing your friends are. I'm sure it's not from your Mum. If she's like mine, she'll have no idea how to text.'

Toby had not heard from his ex since they had split up so he did not think he would be compromised.

'Go on then. Open it up.' Sophie said looking over his shoulder.

'Okay, fine. Here it is:'

A PUNCTURE. A KEY. A SOLUTION. A FRISSON. YOUR TURN.

'Wow,' said Sophie frowning, 'what a strange text. Who's it from?'

'No idea! Oh no! Wait. I remember. I had a puncture and a kind woman helped me with the key to the wheel's bolt, which I couldn't undo. It must be from her, but that was about three months ago. Her husband is probably away and she is just having some fun. It's nothing really. I don't think I'll even bother replying.' Sophie looked hurt.

'There must have been something between you. No one uses the word "frisson" unless there is a bit of electricity in the air.'

'Well I have to admit she was a beautiful woman, but probably in her late thirties, early forties and so a bit old even for me.' As he said it he did remember what an impression she had made on him over that short period of time. Later he had thought nothing more about it. Although it was a fun text and he might yet reply.

'Is there any "frisson" between you and I?' Sophie said earnestly.

'Of course there is,' but he knew that whilst he liked Sophie a lot, the more he thought about it, the more he remembered that there had been a certain "something" between him and that woman.

'Cheer up Sophie. As you can tell I'd forgotten all about her whilst you are very much on my mind. Come on, let's go out and have some dinner.'

Toby did forget all about it, except over the next few days, he kept having a nagging feeling he should be doing something about something but he had no idea what. It was only after a bit of a Sunday lunchtime session at The Ship, that he remembered her text. Sophie, who was turning out to be good fun, had left his house after breakfast that morning and his two housemates, Robert and Tim, had ribbed him incessantly in the pub about his new "bird". But now he was plugged into his stereo listening to a Scissor Sisters CD, flat out on his bed. After a while he picked up his mobile and re-read Maggie's text.

A PUNCTURE. A KEY. A SOLUTION. A FRISSON. YOUR TURN.

Memories came flooding back and he thought, just for fun, he would reply to it. Also, he would probably catch her serving the family Sunday roast, that is if she kept her mobile near her, or indeed switched on, at the weekend. He needed to be succinct but cute. So he texted:

A CHANCE MEETING. A BUSINESS CARD. A POSSIBLE ADVENTURE?

It felt cool, so he sent it off right away and carried on listening to his CD. Imagine his surprise when his mobile beeped and he saw:

Message received.

He was surprised how disappointed he was when he found out it was from Sophie thanking him for last night. Now he had sent Maggie the text he was dying for a reply. He received it sooner than he expected, when he was on his way to see some friends that evening, up it popped -

ADVENTUROUS LADY SEEKS YOUNG PORSCHE OWNER. PREFERABLY MALE. NEEDS URGENT HELP.

Maggie had decided to get fruity early to see if she could ensnare him. Now he had texted her she felt a powerful bond between the two of them, as though they were old friends.

And Toby was feeling pretty flattered. Should he continue? Why not? It would be their secret. No one else would know about them. It would be like having their own world, he fantasised, little knowing that was exactly what Maggie, as a fairly happily married woman presumably with kids, wanted. No baggage for either player. Before he went out to see his friends and before he chickened out, he texted her:

YOUNGISH PORSCHE OWNER SEEKS SIMILAR MODEL WITH A VIEW TO COMPARING NOTES ON BIG ENDS, LEATHER AND AND GASKETS. PUNCTURED FROM WANDSWORTH.

Toby got a strange kick out of sending this text which he had never had before. Texting was his way of life but not with someone he hardly knew, who seemed pretty keen.

'Is that another text you've just had Mummy?' enquired her teenage daughter, Diana, 'if I didn't know you better I'd think it was an admirer. None of your business colleagues ever text you, and anyway, it's Sunday.'

'Sorry darling, I seem to have deleted it. It was something to do with winning a holiday in the Algarve. I should be so lucky to have an admirer. Come on, let's get ready to drive back to school and less of your cheek!'

As she drove both her daughters back, she realised she was actually quite excited by his last text, particularly the reference to "big ends", "leather" and " gaskets". Maybe she was reading too much into it, but she was sure she had hooked him, and why not? She needed a bit of excitement, so long as it was on her terms.

During the following week she thought she would "up the ante" a bit and show her hand with an email. That way he would get to know that she worked for a large and successful firm of lawyers, and also it moved the relationship from the restriction of a mobile to an e-mail, which was more personal and more could be said. That Wednesday evening, in early June she stayed late and composed an email:

Your texts have been great. We share the same sense of humour. I do however think you ought to know I'm married with two children but I do love hearing from you. So if you're happy let's, continue with our electronic flirtation. I think it's great fun and I feel younger by the minute and now understand what my daughters go through when they are texted. So, ciao bello. Our secret, OK? Also, tell me a bit about yourself. Maggie xx

Once she had sent it she felt elated, like a girl with a teenage crush.That evening, when she got home, Neil mentioned that she looked different, as if she had won the lottery.

'No darling. I wish. Just working late at the office and getting a few things done I should have done ages ago.'

Like taking on a young lover, she thought recklessly.

'I should be so lucky,' she whispered.

'What did you say, darling?' her husband asked.

'Nothing. Sorry. Just talking to myself again as usual.'

Toby was in a foul mood when he arrived at the office late on Monday morning. He had enjoyed an evening with some old friends, but came back late to a couple of texts from Sophie saying he had promised to ring, and he had said he might take her with him that night. No way he thought. He had just finished a long relationship and did not want a text that morning at nine o'clock from Sophie checking if it was Monday or Tuesday night he was taking her out. Enough's enough, he thought, as he deleted her message. Now it would be neither Monday nor Tuesday. Once in the office he quickly texted her:

VERY BUSY I'LL CALL YOU LATER THIS WEEK.

That should shut her up. He turned on his computer and went into his e-mails. There were at least a dozen, some sent on Friday night from their US office. But one especially caught his eye, that had been sent a few days ago.

Once he opened it again he realised there was no turning back. His heart was beating madly with excitement at the prospect that, if he played his cards right, he might see her again. He emailed her right away:

It's Monday morning and I was not a happy man until I read your email. Our electronic relationship is now officially up and running. I'm 26 single and a Libran, living

in Wandsworth with a couple of guys and just dying to see you again. I can always do lunch. Ciao Bella. Toby xx

Once he had written it and sent it, he felt as if there was a new purpose to his life. He came down to earth, pretty quickly when, within a few minutes, she had replied:

I love it when you romance me with words. I'm a lawyer, and also a Libran. I was thinking ultimately of something a little more personal than lunch!! M xx

She's a cool customer, Toby thought. Certainly a "come-on" email although he appreciated now that he mustn't rush. He also felt tormented thinking about, and trying to remember, exactly what she looked like during those short ten minutes. The stakes were now raised, as more could be said by email, but more importantly he knew where she worked - Aylmer and Partners. And just as luck would have it one of his university chums, Dave Allen, worked there. He had not seen him for a couple of months but he'd certainly be seeing him now in the next couple of days.

Toby had a lot on that morning, and it wasn't until he arrived home that he was able to call Dave.

'Dave speaking.'

'Hi Dave, it's Toby Jones.'

'Toby! Great to hear from you. How are you?'

'Fine. Fine. Any chance of a drink sometime later this week? I've got something I want to talk to you about.'

'Bet it's a woman as usual,' Dave said laughing, 'let's say Thursday evening seven o'clock at The Coopers Arms, Flood Street. OK?'

'Cool. Thanks. See you then!' and Toby rang off. He just

couldn't wait. Just as he was leaving his mobile beeped with a text:

NIGHT NIGHT SLEEP TIGHT DON'T LET THE BUGS BITE IF THEY CRAWL DON'T SQUALL TAKE A SPOON AND EAT THEM ALL. SWEET DREAMS M XXX

Toby's heart was pounding as he lay in bed trying to get to sleep. Her message was exactly the same as the one his grandmother always said when she was putting him to bed. What a coincidence. He sent her a brief text the following morning:

NOT BITTEN BY BUGS. ONLY BY YOU. KEEP SMILING. ME X

He didn't really want to commit himself any further at this stage until he met Dave on Thursday. Just before he left for home late that Tuesday evening Maggie emailed:

Your electronic friend. People say my bark is worse than my bite. Well, woof, woof!! Will you take me walkies or have you something else in mind? M xxx

Maggie smiled when she sent this email. Having originally wanted a slow electronic romance as no more than a bit of fun, she now knew she wanted him. Just this innocent flirting had turned her on. Things needed to move much more quickly. She couldn't stop thinking about him. Her body ached at night yearning for him to be with her, touching her all over. Late Wednesday night, Simon texted her:

I AM FULLY TRAINED & WILL DO TRICKS. T X

That should do it, he thought. He was now definitely interested. And Thursday evening couldn't arrive soon enough.

Trick or treat. I do both! Watch your post. Could be steaming. With love from your Maggie- in- waiting x

This email had arrived just before he had left his office on Thursday. He did not quite get it but if it was "post" as in "mail" things were progressing nicely.

Over a pint or two Dave brought him up to date with his girlfriend, work and other friends, and then said,

'Enough of me. Lovely to see you and all that, but you did sound a bit desperate. I hope you didn't want to see me on a professional basis.'

'No! No! Not at all. It's just that I have met, but this must remain between you and I, a lady from your practice who is pretty senior I imagine, and we've been texting and emailing and I just need your advice on what to do next. It's all great fun and innocent at the moment, but I'd quite like to take it further. Her name is Maggie Ward.'

'Wow! How on earth did you meet her? She's a very glamorous woman who is one of our top international lawyers. I would imagine she's earning over a quarter of a million a year.'

'Fine! Fine! But what is she actually like?'

'Very popular. Her door is always open. I've often asked her for advice. She's one of those people that whenever you talk to her you know she's concentrating on you and nothing else. Every so often she's out and about in Europe, only calling in at the firm maybe once or twice a week. From what I can gather she's fairly happily married to a rather unsuccessful City guy, and has a couple of girls in their early teens away at school. Apart from that, and the fact that she's one of the best-looking and nicest women I've ever met, except for Mum obviously, I don't know much else about her. She's certainly not an old "woofer"!' Simon grimaced at the word, remembering her last email.

'So now tell me! What's your interest in her?' Dave asked, intrigued and Toby answered in detail.

'Go for it, mate, that's my advice. She's probably a bit frustrated and is looking for an affair with a younger man. One thing I'm sure of, she's a class act and she'd be very discreet. There's never been any rumour about her on that front. So good luck. "Sup up" Yorkshire style, and I'll buy you another pint.'

'Thanks mate,' Toby replied somewhat smugly for obvious reasons.

Earlier that day Maggie had been in a card shop, looking for a birthday card for her younger daughter. She was amazed at how crudely funny some cards had become, and there was one that particularly caught her eye. This card, she thought, could quickly personalise their electronic relationship and hopefully speed up the denouement which she was now longing for.

Following his drink with Dave, Toby went home and thought long and hard about Maggie. He liked the fact that she was older and so far had made most of the running. What worried him was getting into a relationship with a married woman. Somehow he did not think that would happen with the constraints of her family. That being so, if something was going to happen he was happy for it to be covert and on her terms.

The next morning, Toby was busy at his desk, when he noticed amongst his post and memos in his in-tray a bright blue envelope. He picked it up, and it was marked "Private and Confidential". He quickly tore it open. It showed a couple in bed with the man reading the "Kama Sutra" whilst the woman was engrossed in "Great Expectations". Cool, he thought. Inside it said,

'How supple are you? I need some magic - M x,'

He had a great answer to that one. Round the corner from his office was a shop that sold magic tricks etc., so he went there during his lunch break and purchased a wand. Unfortunately it was Friday, so she would not get it and his message until Monday morning. For the moment he emailed her:

Card cool. I'm afraid I'm not a magician but I can always learn and I will just for you. Have a great weekend and roll on Monday. Toby x

Her reply was instant:

If music be the food of love please play on and on and on and on! Who knows what magic there is between us.

PS It's been only a week and I feel as though I've known you for a long and glorious time. xx

Toby was now in the mood. He desperately needed to at least talk to Maggie, and set up a meeting. He made up a special card for her with the wand stuck on the front with the words.

"I HAVE ANOTHER MAGIC WAND I'D LOVE TO WAVE IN FRONT OF YOU!"

And inside was his direct line into Technophile. He posted it to her that evening and spent the whole weekend nervously waiting for Monday morning. But no call, text or email until at 5.30 pm, she finally called.

'Toby Jones speaking.'

'Hello Toby, it's me, Maggie.' Her voice was husky and his nerves taut.

'Hi, how are you?'

'Fine. I need to see you and I think it's mutual. Yes?'

With his voice cracking slightly Toby replied, 'Very much so. But where and when?'

'Let's have a drink on Wednesday evening to settle our nerves and take stock. Do you know Gerrard's Bar in Notting Hill? I've never been there, but apparently it's very intimate and discreet which should suit us. Also it's far enough away from Chelsea and Wandsworth, if you get my meaning.'

'Yeah! That's fine. Are you sure about this?'

'Why? Aren't you? I hope you haven't been stringing me along. I fancied you when I met you. I've enjoyed our correspondence over the last week and I'd like to see you again. Although I'm older than you, this isn't a thing I've ever done before, so I'm probably just as nervous as you. So let's say six thirty on Wednesday at Gerrard's Bar. Ciao bello,' and she rang off.

The next day at lunch, with a few of his workmates, Toby asked if anyone had been to Gerrard's Bar.

'Yes I have,' said Annie, 'it has very subdued lighting, banquette seats and it's considered to be a lovers' paradise. Are you offering to take me then?'

'No, sorry. I just wondered,' Toby replied.

'Make sure your handbag's full. It's extremely expensive,' she replied.

Back at his desk there was an email from Maggie. Rather formal, he thought disappointedly.

Bar Gerrard, Greenstone Street, Notting Hill. Six thirty tomorrow. Please be on time, because I just can't wait. Maggie x x

He replied:

Can't wait. Thrilled to bits. Won't be late. Is this fate?

Straightaway he received:

Sorry last email rather formal. Very busy but also can't wait and I'm never late. It should be fun. Hope you're straight?! You never know! Maggie x x

Toby felt over the moon and Maggie ten years younger as they both considered their illicit rendezvous.

The following evening, he arrived early but she was already there. He noticed as she got up to greet him, her well-cut suit, her amazing figure but most of all her face. Short blonde hair, lips to die for and cool grey eyes.

'Hi Toby,' she said hugging him and then kissing him on both cheeks. 'I've ordered some Bolly. Come and sit next to me and tell me all about yourself. But first, here's to us and whatever happens, happens.'

Toby felt relaxed, and soon the Bolly took over and he told her all about his childhood, his parents and his younger sisters, a bit about his gap year and university and then on to the present. All the while she held him with her gaze, her cool eyes dancing in the dim light.

'So there you have it,' he said, at last. 'Your turn now.'

'Okay. But only up to your age, which I was when I was married.' She was a great storyteller and he was captivated, and wished he had been old enough to have been in Klosters when she was a chalet girl, or Avignon when she was an au pair, or Majorca when she was a sailing instructor. Hell, he thought, now doesn't come much better!

'So enough of me. Please look at me and tell me what you see.'

'A gorgeous woman, impossibly beautiful, who is unfortunately married, but perhaps needs some excitement in her life. I'm sorry, I'm confused. I've said too much. But you really are something else.'

'So, Toby, if I said I feel the same about you, but, of course, you're not married, what are you going to do about it?' she asked, raising her eyebrows.

'Me? Well...'

'I've an idea,' she said interrupting. 'I don't expect to figure in your social life, so please don't worry about the older woman. But in your sex life, I think I could make you and me very, very happy.' As she said this she pulled his head towards her and kissed him urgently at the same time caressing his chest with her long, firm fingers. Minutes seemed to fly by and she then whispered.

'Come out to my car. I've got a proposition to make,' and she got up and left, with him following a little awkwardly behind her. She held his hand as they walked along the pavement.

Once they were in her car, he smothered her with kisses and delicately traced a line with his fingers along the inside of her thighs up to her crotch.

'Mm.... that's lovely but not - oh yes! Touch me there Caress me. Feel me. See, I need you! No more, no more, you'll have me screaming. Now, let's get down to business. I think we have established we want each other. No, no, I said no more- ooh ooh!' she moaned, 'please please no more. Just listen to me for a moment,'

Toby was in seventh heaven. He had never met someone who turned him on so much. And he just could not keep his hands off her.

'Okay. I'm sitting on my hands.'

'Good. But not for too long, darling,' she replied. 'My proposition is this. I can't for many reasons be your girlfriend, but I want, and need, to be your lover. No please. Oh! Oh! No more no more. Put your seat belt on and stop it for goodness sake! Now Toby, I spend a lot of time away on business in Europe, travelling from London mostly to European capital cities. And as I'm the senior partner serving those European clients, I can come and go as I please. What if we meet once a week at an airport hotel, be it Heathrow or Gatwick, at seven-ish, and make mad, passionate love through the night and then we both get off to work? Even better, if we meet for breakfast, and do it through the day and you get home to your place and me to mine and it looks as if I've done a day trip. Probably that's a better idea, if you can get the time off.'

Toby was stunned, but loved the idea.

'Actually I'm often away myself on business at the

weekends so have weekdays off in lieu. I like the idea of a day's love-making, as that way our own lives are not affected.'

'Great, so it's a deal. Let's kiss on it. Oh, oh! that's fabulous.' After a few minutes she came up for air and said, 'You must, must go before I jump on you. I'll email you, so we can get some dates in our diaries. I don't think I've ever felt so horny. Come here one last time.'

The following morning Toby sat at work with a huge grin on his face. Everyone remarked on how happy he looked.

Maggie meanwhile had warned her husband that she would be away on business in Europe a lot during the next few months.

'So what's new?' he said, 'just don't tire yourself out, darling.' What does he know she thought, smiling to herself. I should be so lucky. Later she texted Toby:

DARLING. RADISSON INTERNATIONAL AT HEATHROW. THIS WEDNESDAY. MY TREAT. SEVEN PM IN THE BAR. KISSES M XXXXX

He replied:

CAN'T WAIT. MINE'S A DRY MARTINI TOBY XXXXXXXXX

And so it finally comes to pass. They meet in the bar. They drink and then they go up to the room. He uses the card and unlocks the door. She throws down her bag and he dims the lights. They reach the bed quickly as he pulls back the covers. Breathing deeply they both stand there kissing as she moves her hand through his clothes undoing his shirt, throwing it aside, and feeling the hard smoothness of his back as he lifts off her top and flicks open her bra. Confusion reigns with hard kisses and fumbling of clothes as they eventually intertwine naked on the bed. They lie side by side, hands exploring each other while kissing and licking in a frenzy. She touches him gently, pulling him towards her. He slips inside her and joins his body to hers as if they were one.

And so they progressed with their passionate love making, through that night and many more nights and many more days. Over the next few months they stayed in as many different hotels as possible, to keep their anonymity. Their sex lacked nothing. Both were fulfilled, and neither wanted any more than just that in the relationship. This was slightly more difficult for Toby to come to terms with at first, but the sex was so good he was prepared to take it all at face value. Or something like that. He carried on with his life and she with hers.

Everything would have been fine, except that her husband had noticed she'd spent a lot of time "away on business" during the last few months.

Her firm had no worries, as she was still bringing in the "bacon", big time, but her husband had, once or twice, commented on the amount of time she was away.

One evening, after Maggie had been seeing Toby at least once or twice a week for the last few months, Neil suggested that they take a trip to New York before Christmas to do some shopping and use up some of her Air Miles.

With his minuscule income and Maggie having to pay the school fees, there was not much money left. However, a couple of years ago, her Air Miles had flown them to New York for free, and even paid for the hotel.

'Yes, that's a great idea,' she'd replied and thought no

more about it until a few days later, after another blissful session with Toby, when Neil said to her over dinner in a quiet and threatening voice, most unlike him.

'I should have guessed. You've been on a high these last few months, and I innocently put it down to work. I must have been missing something, because when I phoned your firm today to check on your Air Miles for our trip to New York, they said, and I quote, "You'll be lucky to get to Edinburgh". I have to say I was a little surprised as, according to your diary, which I have here,' Toby started shouting hysterically, 'you've been to Rome, Paris, Madrid, Frankfurt, Copenhagen, Lisbon, Innsbruck, Geneva, Bonn, Milan, Vienna, Edinburgh, Copenhagen, Barcelona, Nice, Amsterdam, Venice, Stockholm, Marseilles, Zurich, Bordeaux, St Petersburg, Florence, Barcelona, Munich, Dublin, Berlin, Vienna, Glasgow and all points North, South, East and West during the last few months!! But it would appear that you have not accrued any Air Miles at all.'

Now Neil spoke softly, in an angry and menacing voice.

'So, where exactly have you been, you trans-European, two-timing, frequent-traveller bitch!? I'm dying to know!'

PROBABLY THE ULTIMATE PRANK

From the time he could walk and then talk, Charlie Adams had been a practical joker. Call him what you will, he was a prankster extraordinaire, indulging in all types of pranks to include horseplay, jokes, skylarking, high jinks, tomfoolery - you name them, he did them. It took his mother, Mary, a long time to realise that their dog, Bonzo, ate most of Charlie's food when he didn't feel like eating it. And he was just two years old, at the time!

So that was just the beginning. His jokes and pranks, some more obvious than others, really got going when he went to boarding school. If it wasn't apple-pie beds or tying shoe laces together, it was setting off the fire alarm in the middle of the night, or feigning illness to get off a Latin exam. He also kept his hand in during the holidays. He once waited under his grandmother's bed until she had turned her light off, then jumped out, wailing like a banshee. They reckoned she aged ten years that night. Then there was a Valentine's Day when he sent a card to his father with just xxxxxxxx on it. He knew his mother thought his father was up to no good, coming home later and later from work. It caused all sorts of emotional problems, with father vehemently denying it and Charlie smirking and fuelling the fire as they argued.

Strangely they never suspected Charlie, as he was only nine at the time although he also enjoyed phoning home from his friends' in the evening and ringing off as soon as his mother answered, which perplexed her no end. After a while he tired of this kind of tomfoolery, and his parents, once again, settled into their normal routine.

When he was thirteen, he was sent off to Goodwood House , a minor public school in Sussex, and it was there that he became best of friends with Harry Sinclair. Now Harry was a very different character to Charlie. He was good at everything; exams and sport, drama and music and popular with the staff and boys alike. In fact he was an all-round good egg, and surprisingly put up with Charlie and his endless horseplay.

'You're amazing, Harry,' Charlie once said. 'You never seem fazed by my endless pranks, or even bother to retaliate.'

'I'd certainly not retaliate, otherwise you would probably double your efforts,' he said, laughing, 'and anyway, someone has to be the butt of your endless skylarking and I can take it. In a perverse way I quite enjoy waiting for your next trick. As long as they're harmless, who cares?'

'You're probably right. That trick I played on Henderson minor backfired a bit. Having to write five thousand words on "Silence Is Golden" was not my idea of a fun punishment. But wait until next term. I've got a cracking prank I'm planning, and it only affects you indirectly. For the rest of this term, I'll conserve my energy,' and so saying he and Harry rushed off to the tuck shop before it closed.

During the following term, their chemistry teacher, old man Donaldson, was taking the fourth form through all the acids and their make-up, inter-relationships and eventual practical use.

Charlie and Harry, being inseparable, were sitting together at the back of the laboratory.

'Now listen, children. This sample of acid, in fact, looks and tastes like very bitter lemon juice. So I'm going to pass round this crucible, please come and take it Sinclair, and will each of you just touch the liquid with your little finger and then taste it.'

'Heck! He's quite right you know, Charlie. Here, try it!' Harry said. Whereupon Charlie picked up the crucible and swallowed all of it, in one go, sat bolt upright and collapsed, inert, on the floor.

'Sir! Sir! Adams has drunk the whole lot,' Johnson minor shouted across the laboratory.

'Oh my God!' said Donaldson, rushing over. 'One of you ring 999 now and tell the emergency services to send an ambulance round right away. Now four of you carry Adams quickly to the North Front where the ambulance should arrive shortly.'

'I got through, sir. I briefly told them what had happened and the paramedics will be here in ten minutes,' said Johnson, relishing his role.

'One of you get some blankets from somewhere to keep Adams warm,' shouted Donaldson, now in quite a panic as the enormity of what had happened hit home. He had been doing this practical exercise for years and years, but never this. "Oh my God!" he thought, " I just hope he survives."

Adams was meanwhile being carried to the front hall of the school, wrapped in a blanket and propped up in a chair. He did not look good and his breath was coming in short gasps.

'Sir, will he survive?' Harry asked anxiously.

'I just don't know. Once the acid gets into his nervous system, his liver or kidneys, who knows what the damage could be.'

'Sir, sir, I can hear the ambulance's siren,' Johnson cried, which was more than poor old man Donaldson did as he was pretty deaf and the poor master was now looking pale and worried sick.

'Move away, please,' said one of the paramedics as they gently lowered Adams onto a stretcher.

'I'd like one of the boys to accompany us please, and could you, sir, jot down in this notebook exactly what the acid was. Thank you. Now please, all stand back.'

Soon the ambulance was speeding away from the school with Charlies's best friend, Harry, holding his hand and mopping his brow. Imagine his, and the paramedics' surprise, when Charlie sat bolt upright, smiled and said:

'I substituted the acid with squeezed lemon juice. So, there you have it, I live and so does today, April 1st. I've fooled a few people, I believe.'

The reaction of the paramedics was unprintable and Harry, although relieved, was not impressed. Nor was Mr Symonds, the headmaster, who rusticated Charlie for the rest of the term, with an enormous flea in his ear and promised that if anything similar occurred, he would be expelled.

Strangely, Charlie's parents, who were used to his pranks, took it in good spirit.

'It wasn't an original prank because I'm sure I've read about it somewhere, but, nevertheless, do heed the headmaster's advice, Charles, okay?' his father said.

'Yes, Dad, I will. I promise'

And Charlie kept his promise through school apart from

occasional minor pranks, such as kidnapping his house matron's dog and demanding a ransom, or hiding all the boys' hymn books in chapel for a couple of days, forcing the masters to sing on their own.

Charles and Harry still remained great friends, although Harry, since the acid affair, was a little apprehensive as to what Charlie might have in store - for him.

They both went to Bristol University, where Charlie found it more difficult to carry on with his horseplay. It had somehow been appropriate at school, but not at university. However, to keep his hand in, Charlie once again targeted his friend Harry. At one of the Saturday night bottle parties, Charlie filled up an empty bottle of red wine with ink and water and proudly presented it to Harry, who was well gone.

'Hi Harry you look really pissed. Here's an unusual red you'll enjoy. I've already opened it so drink it straight from the bottle.'

'Thanks me old mucker, I will,' and so saying proceeded to miss his mouth and pour blue ink all over his face, hands and shirt. Not a pretty sight. Charlie howled with glee but Harry sobered up quickly, clearly not impressed. Charlie beat a hasty retreat.

'Wait until I see you again, you bastard, Charlie,' was all Charlie could hear as he hot footed it down the stairs of Harry's hall of residence.

His opportunity for revenge came during that summer vac., when they were both staying at a friend's house, following a 21st birthday party the previous evening. Both were severely hungover. There were about a dozen people sitting round the swimming pool, nursing headaches, prior to the first Bloody Marys promised for midday. For once

Charlie was minding his own business, sitting on a chair by the pool reading the Sunday Times. Harry saw his opportunity and with the help of one of his friends picked Charlie up, paper and all, and flung him in the deep end, laughing uncontrollably.

'That'll teach him.'

Everyone had got up to look and laugh, but imagine their horror when Charlie's body just lay there on the bottom of the pool for what seemed like ages.

'Come on,' said Harry to his mate Nick. 'This looks serious. Let's go in and pull him out.' Which they did, laying him out gently beside the pool. He lay there, very still, and then suddenly smiled, and took in a huge breath of air.

'That fooled you. I can stay underwater for three minutes, without floating to the surface, if I exhale completely. I heard you coming up behind me so I had enough time to empty my lungs. Fooled you all and look, here come the Bloody Marys.'

Whereupon, with Harry's and Nick's eyes on the bearer of the drinks tray, Charlie pushed them both into the pool.

As the terms went by Charlie's pranks continued, although they were mainly reserved for his so-called friend Harry.

Perhaps the most aggravating one involved a game of golf with high stakes. Both men were good players. If anything Harry was the better of the two. He laid down a £100 challenge that Charlie and his golfing mate from home, Dave Sutton, could not beat him and his fellow club member, Michael. The reason for the wager was that Charlie had gone on and on about how he and David Sutton had won the Four Ball competition at their club for the last three years. In the end, Harry and his friend Michael duly beat

Charlie and David but, as they were coming off the 18th green, Charlie casually enquired on the number of golf clubs in Harry's bag.

'What are you blathering about? Look we beat you fair and square. One hundred quid from each of you please,' Harry replied crossly.

'Well I'm not so sure. It looks to me as if you've got one wedge too many, probably taking you over the fourteen clubs limit.'

'I'm sorry, Harry, but I think Charlie's right. I can see fifteen clubs in your bag' said David.

'Our match I believe. Sorry old chap, must have slipped your mind. One hundred each for us please,' Charlie said making his way to the clubhouse.

'Michael, I'm so sorry. I can't imagine how that happened. I'll pay your hundred quid' Harry offered.

He could have started with fifteen clubs but he reckoned he would have noticed. Surely even Charlie would not pull off a prank like that. Or would he? Again Harry gave him the benefit of the doubt, and even asked him to make a speech at his 21st later that summer.

'Please keep it clean, and no pranks.' This 21st was a dinner dance at a hotel, and some members of Harry's family and friends were staying there overnight. Neither Harry nor Charlie had special girlfriends, just lots of friends who were girls. They found themselves alone after everyone had left, in the hotel bar, which was still open.

'Thanks for your speech. It was excellent, and also for no pranks.'

'Pleasure's all mine Harry.'

Over the next half an hour Harry made quite a play for the very attractive Swedish barmaid, and kept telling her what his room number was. Meanwhile, Sue, the other barmaid, was hatching a plot with Charlie. Obviously she was a fellow joker, because she suggested she and Charlie clear everything out of Harry's room. It was something they often did at the hotel if someone was getting fresh and suggestive.

'I get it. So Ingrid closes up the bar, tells Harry to wait five minutes, giving her time, in his mind, to be lying in his bed waiting for him.'

'Of course. She unlocks his door, leaving the key in the door for Harry and she then goes off to her own room. The only downside for us is we can't actually get to see his face, although Ingrid and I are on duty at breakfast so we can all ask him if he had a good night.'

'Wait a sec. I love it, but I must see his face. You say goodnight to Harry and me now, then Ingrid joins you and can you then move the furniture out? I'll stall Harry and come up to his room and wish him luck. That way it's your prank not mine, and I get to see the expression on his face. And also, to be fair, he can sleep in my room. He is my mate after all!'

'Good thinking. I've already briefed Ingrid and she's up for it. We've done it before so no probs.'

'How are you two lovebirds getting on?' Charlie asked casually

'Well Ingrid's agreed to be my birthday present. Haven't you, darling?'

'Oh yes, you bet, you lovely twenty-one year old man. Let me close up the bar and Harry, darling, I'll meet you in your room, number twenty one, in ten minutes. Okay? I'm sure your friend can look after you,' she said smiling.

Harry and Charlie followed about ten minutes later and

Charlie said, nudging him.

'Well here's your room me old mucker. Go on in and enjoy Ingrid, this could be a memorable 21st present.' He was in and out, quick as a flash!

'What the F**k's going on, Charlie. Is this another of your facile pranks or what?'

'Sorry, nothing to do with me, I assure you.' Charlie said as he went into a very empty room.

'Wow! I've been out-pranked. They must have been in this together. Cool girls. Let's go to my room, it's got twin beds. Anyway wait till you see Ingrid tomorrow. She wasn't that great anyway.'

'F**k you, Charlie! It's got your hallmark'

'No way was it me. I was with you all the time, remember? Very probably they pull this prank a few times a year. Come on, bedtime, and stop swearing at me. Bad luck you're going to have to sleep with me tonight and I promise you I didn't do it, although I'm very impressed!'

'Sorry, Charlie, sorry. Even you wouldn't deny a guy a lay would you?'

'No comment. Let's get you off to bed,' Charlie said guiding a very drunk and maudlin Harry towards his room.

At breakfast the next morning Charlie said:

'I'm upset that you think I had anything to do with last night's fiasco. So much so that I want it put on record that after that prank, which was brilliant, the prankster is officially dead,' so saying Charlie took Harry's hand and shook it hard. 'By the way, no sign of Ingrid or Sue this morning,' he quipped.

'Thank God! No more pranks. You really mean it?' Harry enquired, not believing a word of it.

'Absolutely. Unless of course....'

'Come on make up your mind, please. I can't stand the tension.'

'Okay. I'll be straight. If I can dream up a better one than last night, I might have one more go.'

'Well please not at my expense, if you don't mind.'

'We'll see.'

And that was that. For a while Harry and Charlie saw little of each other. After university, Charlie went to work in New York, whilst Harry got a job in the City. Charlie returned to London after three years and their friendship blossomed again, particularly as Harry was going steady with a girl called Pippa who they had both known at university. Also there had been no more pranks since Harry's 21st.

A couple of years later, Charlie had a phone call from Harry.

'Please come for dinner at my flat Tuesday week with Laura. Pippa and I have a little announcement to make.' Laura was Charlie's long-standing girlfriend.

'Come on, Pippa's not pregnant is she Harry? That would be some prank!'

'Don't be silly. Just wait and see. Till next Tuesday then,' and Harry put the phone down.

You've guessed it reader. They'd got engaged, and Harry asked Charlie to be his best man.

'But remember,' said Pippa, 'No pranks. I remember your reputation at university and Harry was reminding me about what happened at his 21st. So promise, hand on heart, nothing at his stag night, my hen night or particularly at the wedding itself.'

'I promise. You know I'm a reformed character. Almost grown-up! I told Harry after his 21st that I'd do one more prank only if it's much better than all my other efforts.

'Are you sure?' Pippa asked looking Charlie straight in the eye. 'Nothing until after the wedding and we're out of the country.'

'As God is my witness. I'll shake on it with all three of you to show I'm serious.'

'How on earth can you promise not to disrupt something? I mean, after all, everyone I've ever met who's known you over the years always bangs on about your tomfoolery, and more often than not, have been pretty impressed with what you've done in the past. It's now six and a bit years since Harry's 21st and nothing. Why?' Laura asked.

'Well I made a promise then, and also Americans might not have found my pranks all that amusing. But mainly because I've grown out of it all,' Charlie replied.

Laura implored. 'I know you really well, probably better than anyone else except your family and Harry, and it's just not like you to pass up a stag and hen night and the wedding itself. The opportunities are endless, aren't they?'

'Yes, but I can't anymore. I gave my word. Anyway I'll have a lot on my plate organising the stag party, ushers, my wedding speech etc. etc. I promised only one more and it needn't necessarily be played out on Harry and Pippa. It could be you Laura!' Charlie said laughing.

'You wouldn't dare would you?' Laura retorted.

'Trust me. I would,' Charlie replied in a serious tone that made Laura realise he certainly would.

Charlie kept to his word, organising a pretty grown-up stag party. It was a black tie affair with cocktails and dinner in a private room at his club, the In and Out, and then on to a club in Soho for some gambling, and later, affairs of the heart for those interested.

Earlier that afternoon, Charlie had had a call from Harry's

fiancée pleading.

'Please, please send him back in one piece. You promised.'

'There will be no tomfoolery tonight. Have a good hen "do", but keep an eye on Laura. I think she's hatching something, sorry about the pun. It's contagious you know,' he said laughing.

'Oh no, not her as well.'

'My lips are sealed. Have a good one.'

Much, much later, sometime around dawn. Harry and Charlie were having a final nightcap.

'Thanks for organising the evening, Charlie. It went well, and no pranks.'

'It's not quite over yet,' Charlie said and Harry visibly blanched.

'It's OK. I'm only joking. Next up the wedding and then you jet off to Barbados on the Monday where you'll be staying at the Sandy Lane Hotel, which I know you'll love.'

'Yes, thanks for recommending it. I've "googled" the hotel and it looks fantastic. It's just a shame we can't leave until Sunday, but as you know, Anna's parents have insisted on a barbecue for family and friends. They did want you and Laura to come, but you've got some charity do in Dorset'

'Yeah that's right - sorry'

'Don't worry, I think you're well out of it. How is the speech going?' Harry asked, slurring slightly. It had been a long night.

'Nearly finished, and no smutty jokes so don't worry.'

And he didn't. The wedding went like clockwork. Harry took Charlie and the ushers out to lunch where drink was actually rationed. Charlie kept feeling for the ring in his inner pocket. The sun shone. The church was beautiful, the bride stunning and the bridesmaids - cute! Drinks were held in Pippa's parents' lovely Queen Anne house with a marquee attached, followed by dinner, speeches and dancing.

Charlie's speech was witty and urbane, never touching on any of the japes perpetrated by him on the bridegroom.

Later on in the evening, Pippa asked Charlie for a dance.

'I'd love to, Pippa. You look radiant,' he said as they walked towards the dance floor already full of guests dancing to a slow, romantic number.

'Charlie, I have to say I've done you an injustice. I told all my friends how worried I was about you being Harry's best man. I'll even forgive you for the male stripograms you and Laura organised for my hen night. Actually they were very fit. But you have been a brick and really helped Harry out. So, a big kiss and thank you so much. You really have turned out to be a good and loyal friend.'

'Well thank you. I've enjoyed my responsibilities and of course Harry and I go back a long, long way.'

'Do you know, Charlie,' Pippa said smiling 'I'm quite looking forward to your last and final prank. That's of course as long as it's after tonight, because you're off to a charity do tomorrow, aren't you? So hopefully you'll be keeping your promise.'

'Absolutely. My final prank will be after the wedding is done and dusted I promise.'

'Do let me know when it is then I can join in the merriment!' she said laughing.

'Don't worry. You'll certainly know about it. Now, come on, let's go and have a glass of bubbly.'

The rest of the evening went off without a hitch. Fireworks before eleven o'clock, politically correct, and dancing until dawn by which time Harry and Pippa had quietly slipped away.

The barbecue on Sunday was a big success, and Pippa's mother, Jane, was feeling much more relaxed. She had been told all about Charlie and had not been pleased when Harry had asked him to be his best man. She had feared the worst, but now, as she sat by the pool late that Sunday afternoon, she thought how well he had behaved, and what an excellent job he had made of being best man. Her son-in-law was lucky to have such a good friend.

Which was exactly what Harry was saying to Pippa as they lay in bed on the first morning of their honeymoon in Barbados.

'I told you he wouldn't let us down darling. He made a promise and he has kept to it. Let's decide what we're going to have for breakfast. I fancy some fresh orange juice, bacon and eggs, toast and coffee. What about you?'

'Ditto for me please,' she said kissing him lightly on the forehead. 'I'm such a lucky woman.'

'Oh hello, is that room service? Great. Please could I order breakfast for Room 236? I'd like fresh orange juice, bacon and eggs sunny side up, toast and coffee. Sorry? Yes, for two please.'

'Make that for three would you please Harry?' came an unmistakable voice from under the bed!

EDDYSTONE

The Eddystone Lighthouse is generally agreed to be the most famous lighthouse in the world. Some thirteen miles south west of Plymouth and nine miles south of Rames Head, three ridges of viciously hard, red rocks rise from the sea. They have been broken and shattered by the ceaseless pounding of the waves. Only on the calmest of days is the lighthouse approachable, while in rough weather the conditions can be positively evil. The notoriety of this group of rocks has long been known; the pounding seas rip through the narrow channels, causing a turmoil of currents between those rocky teeth, known by the local seafarers as "eddy-stones".

The history of this terrifying cluster of rocks, and the lighthouses placed upon them, is a testament to the bravery and courage of those men who laboured under indescribable conditions to provide light and warning signals to passing ships.

The first Eddystone Lighthouse was built by Henry Winstanley in 1698 and improved and enlarged the following year. This was sadly toppled by the great storm of 1703, but in 1709 another one was built by John Rudyard. Constructed in oak, it caught fire and was destroyed in 1755 to be replaced by John Smeaton's concrete block lighthouse completed in 1759. Smeaton's lighthouse was meant was to last over 125 years, only to be dismantled in 1882 to make way, on a nearby reef, for James Douglass's lighthouse which was almost twice the height of its predecessor at 51 metres, and is still standing proud today.

Alas, in 1982 Eddystone became fully automated, a sad day in the history of the world's most famous lighthouse, and an even sadder one for Bill Long, who was the last lighthouse keeper to man Eddystone.

The Long family went back over two centuries of lighthouse keeping on Eddystone. It had seemed like home for generations of the family. But finally Bill, at the age of fifty-nine, was pensioned off, and went to live with his wife in the little village of Heybrook Bay, just south of Plymouth. On a clear day and at night, weather permitting, he had a clear view of his beloved Eddystone. Interestingly the locals referred to the lighthouse as "Bill's baby", which amused Bill no end.

Twenty years have now elapsed and Bill was looking forward to his grandson, Tom, aged ten, coming to stay. He'd always been Bill's favourite and could do no wrong, particularly if Tom asked him to tell stories about his time on the Eddystone Lighthouse.

'What time is young Tom arriving, Annie?' Bill asked his wife.

'I think Edward's's dropping him off sometime after lunch.'

'Good. That'll give me time to take him fishing before supper.'

Since retiring, Bill had built himself a garden shed, where he kept all his mementoes of Eddystone, and where he dabbled in carpentry. It had been his wife's idea to keep him busy after his retirement.

'You eat, breath and sleep Eddystone, so why don't you put your carpentry skills to good use and make wooden models of the lighthouse?' his wife had asked him one day, shortly after his retirement.

Bill thought this was a grand idea and got to work immediately. Over the years, he had established a good little business constructing and painting Eddystone lighthouses, from nine inches high to his largest which, at over 3 feet tall, was commissioned by Trinity House to celebrate the automation of the last British lighthouse, Fair Isle South, in 1998.

Later that evening, after a successful fishing trip, Tom started asking his Grandpa about Eddystone. The boy never seemed to tire of questioning him about his days as a lighthouse keeper.

'I'm sure I've told you all the stories I can remember Tom.'

'No Grandpa, I've never really understood the actual signals themselves. You once mentioned a Frenchman called Fresnel I think. What did he do?'

'What a memory you've got. I'm impressed,' said Bill, feeling pleased and settling down into his armchair. 'Basically, early in the 19th Century, Augustin, I think that was his Christian name, invented the Fresnel lens. Most lighthouses are equipped with this type of lens, which is a huge compound lens that encircles the lamp. Each face of a Fresnel lens is surrounded by a ring of triangular prisms, which reflect and strengthen the light. Some of these lenses can, in fact, project light over twenty miles, but we were happy with seventeen miles for Eddystone. And tell me, before you go to bed, which should be soon, what's so special about Eddystone's lantern?'

'The double white flash, Grandpa. How could I ever forget that?' He went over to him and gave him a big hug and a kiss for Granny before he went off to bed.

'Such a nice boy, isn't he?' enthused Bill.

'It's just because he listens to your stories so avidly that you like him!' Annie said laughing, 'and don't forget to take the dog out, and say goodnight to your beloved lighthouse.'

As Bill walked along the beach, with his elderly Scottie ambling along behind, he was reassured to see Eddystone flashing in the distance, remembering fondly his times on the lighthouse.

Meanwhile, many miles away, a meeting was being held in a dingy flat in South London.

'Why Plymouth?' asked Dave, a swarthy-looking man in his mid-thirties.

'It's not actually Plymouth but Blackaterry Point, a few miles to the east. It's very isolated and will make an excellent rendezvous, and a quick getaway via Yealmpton and on to the A38 near Ivybridge. We should be back here within three and a half hours,' Peter replied.

There were four of them in the group. Peter was clearly in charge, and besides Dave, there were two others, Mike and Roger. The meeting had been called to discuss the possibility of smuggling cocaine into the country, via a ship, the Silvania, positioned out in the English Channel. Customs and Excise in Cornwall and Devon had, with the local police, tightened up their acts and drug running was becoming increasingly difficult. Peter had recruited his team carefully. All of them had some experience of smuggling, and both Dave and Roger had lived near the proposed dropping-off area, so knew the lie of the land well. Mike had been a local fisherman, and also spent a few months as one of the Eddystone lighthouse's assistant keepers, just prior to it being de-commisioned.

'I'm sure we could just go straight in with the motor cruiser,' said Mike, who was in his late forties, muscle-bound and blond.

'No way, Mike,' Peter replied, 'we've discussed this before. Customs and Excise are stopping more and more boats, and we know for a fact that all the coastline between Penzance and Weymouth is being carefully monitored. They can easily tap into mobile phones. They're also using sophisticated digital radar. However, with a bit of help from a geek friend of mine in London, I think I can now override it without the coast guards having any idea. Don't ask me how it works, but it does. I've been out at sea and tested it. But we need to move quickly as they'll soon cotton on. Now that brings me round to why we're here. As they're clearly getting more sophisticated, we need to surprise them, and do the unexpected. My proposition is that we use the Eddystone Lighthouse.'

'You're joking! The Eddystone Lighthouse? How? Why? It's difficult to get near it even when the sea's calm,' Roger retorted. 'Sorry you're off your nutter!'

'Hang on a minute. Hear me out. As you all know, the Eddystone is unmanned. What I'm proposing is that, instead of doing a number of small runs, which I know you and Dave have been involved in, and which, as you said earlier, is getting more and more risky, we do one big hit. The ship is already on its way from South America, bound for London, and we will rendezvous with it seventeen miles from the lighthouse, so we can just see its beam, but also be far enough away from the mainland. Clearly it will be a big haul, and timing will be crucial. This is where you come in, Mike.'

Mike was much older than the rest of the group, and looked like an old sea dog.

'Wait a minute, Peter. I only worked on Eddystone for a few months.'

'Yes, but you know it well enough. You've always bragged to us how you found your way to the rock once in a RIB in high seas, to deliver essential medical equipment. Even the helicopter wasn't operational that day. I believe you were quite a hero. If you've done it once, I'm sure you can manage it again. Think. This one-off drop will leave you well-off for the rest of your life. Once the coast is deemed clear I want Mike to go into the lighthouse, and change the beam to a triple flash for just two minutes. That will be the signal for us to come in with our RIB and with the booty.'

'I agree,' said Dave. 'It's now far too risky to use motor cruisers.'

'Do you think it can be done Mike?' Peter asked.

'Okay. No bragging. I do believe it can be done, but it will be difficult. For a start I expect the lighthouse to be alarmed, but I should be able to override that. Changing the beam is rather more complex, but I've kept my Eddystone manual so I should be able to manage. I know there are emergency provisions for differing flashes.As I remember, a triple flash is definitely one of them. So before we decide anything, let me just check that out. But I really don't see it as much of a problem,' Mike said.

'Right then. We'll meet up in Devon in a fortnight at The Sloop Inn in Bantham, where I've booked two rooms. So let's meet in the bar at seven o'clock. After dinner we'll go back to my room and fine-tune everything. Mike, give me a buzz on my mobile in the next few days, and let me know how you're getting on,' said Pete.

'Actually,' Mike replied, 'I'll probably slip down to Noss Mayo and stay with my sister next week. Whilst I'm there I'll ask Charlie Wyvill if I can take his fishing smack out for a sail. That way I can get a good look at our way into Eddystone,' Mike replied.

Pete nodded, and the group split up. He was very much the brains behind the project and had been a City broker, but fell on bad times which included a busted marriage, though fortunately no children. Once his redundancy package and ex-wife were sorted, Pete was fairly well off. He had rented a small fisherman's cottage in Newton Ferrers, where he used to holiday as a boy, a couple of years ago. Now he spent every weekend he could there, commuting from his small flat in Stockwell.

Last summer he had bumped into Dave, who he had known when he was a kid and they got talking over a pint, and obviously one thing led to another. Dave and Roger had been involved in quite a lot of small-time drug running over the years which gave Pete some food for thought, but nothing to match what he had later had in mind. Pete's contact for this heist had been made via drug runners, petty criminals and their bosses in the East End of London. His research had been thorough and using various aliases and disguises he had managed to tap into a drug baron, Pedro. He was not a nice man, tough as they come, and ruthless with it. The meetings nearly always took place in hotel bedrooms, with Pedro's two henchmen, Paolo and Giorgio, who you would never want to meet during the day let alone a dark night, standing close by his side. Finally a deal was struck. Pedro would organise the booty from San Paolo on board a cargo ship, the Sylvania. The cocaine would have a street value of £20m in Britain, to be split 50/50 with Pedro. Pete would keep £4m for himself, and split the rest three ways with his team.

Later that week, back in Heybrook Bay, Bill was with his grandson and suggested.

'Seeing as it's such a lovely day, Tom, I think we'll take my yacht out and go and have a look at my old friend Eddystone. I did promise you, didn't I?'

'Oh yes, Grandpa you did! How exciting, I've only been out there once before. When do we go?'

'Just as soon as you have finished your breakfast so we can catch the high tide,' Grandpa replied.

'Now you will be careful, Bill, going to Eddystone. I've never liked you sailing too close. It's one thing being inside, it's quite another sailing near it and round it.'

'Don't worry pet. I'll have a very valuable cargo on board won't I, Tom?'

'You bet Grandpa. I've finished. Let's go!'

'Here are some sandwiches, apples and a Pepsi I've got ready, in case you're peckish,' Annie said.

'Thank you so much Granny,' said Tom and went up to her and gave her a big kiss.

'Now, now, don't get over excited. Just have a good time and look after Grandpa.'

Bill kept his boat over in Newton Ferrers, and on the way over Tom asked if he could take the helm this time, as his Grandpa had promised.

'Okay, once we're out of the harbour you can be skipper for a few minutes while I get the sails ready.'

'Cool Grandpa. Thanks very much.'

Tom got his wish. Once they were under full sail, Bill

took over, and they proceeded swiftly and easily towards Eddystone.

'It looks so small from here Grandpa.'

'You wait until we get nearer. It's very impressive.'

'Tell me about your worst night there again please.' Grandpa was never bored of telling his stories but suddenly he broke off.

'See that fishing boat. It's dangerously near the Eddystone Rocks. Tom, quickly get me my binoculars. Thanks. Take the tiller and keep her on this tack and I'll take a closer look. It looks to me like Nimrod, old Charles Wyvill's boat. I can't understand why he's that close in. Still, he knows these waters like the back of his hand, so I shouldn't worry. Good, he's moving away now. If it had been almost anyone else, I would have been worried. I might give him a ring later on today and see what he was up to. I'll take over now Tom. But well done, you did a good job.'

He did phone Charlie up that evening, and was quite surprised to hear he had been with Mike, whom Bill remembered. Charlie said the trip was for old time's sake and Bill thought no more of it.

'Have you seen enough Mike?' Charlie had asked.

'Yes thanks. Do you remember that time I had to get medical supplies into the lighthouse during that dreadful storm?'

'Of course I do. You were young but quite mad. It's funny though. The lighthouse rightly has a fearsome reputation, but it's not actually that difficult to get to unless it's low tide and there is a significant swell. Only last year some students from Exeter University managed to drop a huge flag round it during Rag Week. Actually, I was quite impressed,' Charlie said, smiling.

'Well since it has been unmanned, I presume Trinity House doesn't want it to be seen as an easy touch, particularly as it's still pretty dangerous to approach, however good the weather.'

'You're absolutely right. Shall we get back now? Your charge for the journey is, as promised, a pie and a pint at the Jolly Sailor.'

'Absolutely,' Mike replied smiling to himself, happy in the knowledge that getting into the lighthouse was, depending on the weather, not going to be too difficult. He could not remember whether Pete had specified a full moon. That would be essential. He would discuss this with him the following week at the Sloop Inn.

The captain of the Sylvania had received a text on his undetectable "pay as you go phone" saying it was too risky for him to pick up Pete and Dave in Cherbourg because too many ships had apparently been docking for specious reasons, alerting the authorities to possible smuggling, and they had clamped down. Pete and Dave would have to get a lift into the English Channel, and meet up with the Sylvania there. The captain was actually quite pleased. He had not been happy about docking at Cherbourg since he had once previously had a problem with the Customs there. And they tend to remember a captain and his ship. So now he needed to work out his timing, rendezvous and drop-off point for his two accomplices, and tie it all in with the new moon. All the same, he was being paid £100,000 for a relatively easy job, so he was not too put out.

'Hi you two, what are you having?' asked Pete as Dave and Roger came into the main bar of The Sloop, a fortnight later.

'Pint of Bass for me Peter. Cheers!' said Dave, 'and Roger

will have a pint of Palmers.'

'Okay. I'm afraid Mike's running a bit late as his aunt's not been too well.'

Mike had phoned Pete the previous evening and told him about his trip with Charlie Wyvill, and that he was happy about getting into Eddystone. He was also confident about changing the beam. It was apparently quite a complex job that would certainly need two people, but it was definitely feasible, and as long as he remembered the manual's instructions, fairly simple.

After the three of them had had a couple of beers, Mike arrived, apologising.

'My poor old aunt. She gets into such a flap if there's anything remotely wrong with her. It's probably why she's still alive at ninety five. Yes, I'd love a pint of Bass.'

It was only small talk during dinner and they finally got down to business about ten o'clock in Pete's room. Pete kept the television on to drown their conversation, even though they talked quietly. There was a general feeling of excitement, tinged with apprehension, but the group was well up for it. Pete kicked off:

'There's been one change of plan. The Sylvania will not be picking us up in Cherbourg. Apparently the French Customs are very tricky and nervous at the moment. Dave, you and I will have to hire a fisherman for the night to get us out into the Channel. I have the rendezvous position. Today's Thursday. Dave, we'll leave tomorrow to give us time to sort things out in Cherbourg. Mike and Roger, you need to be on constant alert this Tuesday, which is when the tide is exactly right, and there is a band of high pressure moving in from the west.'

'What about the full moon?' Dave asked.

'Sorry I forgot, there will of course be a full moon to make life easier. Now Dave and I are up to speed, I can of course keep him briefed as we go along.'

'Well Pete, as I told you on the phone the other day, it looks like Eddystone won't be too much of a problem, and we should be able to adjust the beam for those crucial two minutes, after one o'clock.'

'Great!'

Roger gave Pete chapter and verse of their side of the operation. A RIB had already been bought in Plymouth, and was waiting to be picked up the next day at the city's largest boatyard, where no questions had been asked. Tomorrow it would be moved to Noss Mayo, and left on the quay by the pub. On Monday afternoon the RIB would leave Noss Mayo, ostensibly to go lobster-potting. Upon reaching Blackaterry Point, they would hove to and wait in the shallows out of sight. Once darkness fell both Mike and Roger would don wet suits, and keep watch. If the heist did not happen on that Tuesday they would hide their RIB and pick up the Volvo Estate, motor into Plymouth and lose themselves. They would return at the same time the following evening, as planned.

'Apparently one of the locals in the pub in Noss Mayo says it's like lovers' lane at Blackaterry Point, so an estate car should not cause too much interest. Once it is dark and the coast is clear we'll set off for the lighthouse. When we're inside we'll set up the triple flash to go off as soon as possible after one o'clock.'

'Sounds good, and you two probably know the waters round there better than anyone else I know.'

'Yes, but Eddystone's a different matter,' Mike replied, 'but don't worry we'll cope.'

'Well, now we're all set. I think all the planning has been very thorough, so well done team. Now there's just one other thing I want to discuss. Once we've completed the heist we drive straight back to my flat in London. I'm dealing with a drug baron called Pedro who has two very ugly and tough henchmen. I've insisted that all four of us are together when the pay-off is made. As you know the cocaine is worth at least £20 million with £10 million going to Pedro. £4 million for me and £2 million for each of you. Okay so far?'

They all nodded.

'It will be laundered money and we'll get it there and then. We've all got suits and briefcases back at my flat ready for our meeting. So we can arrive at his specified hotel as businessmen, and leave as rich businessmen.'

They all laughed which eased the tension somewhat.

'I can tell you've got a problem, Pete. What is it?' Mike asked.

'My problem is what you three plan to do with £2m each, in used notes. It's something we've never really discussed, but if one of us gets caught out with a large number of notes, we're probably all for it'

'Why don't you go first, Pete. What will you do?'

'It's slightly easier for me really. As I've always worked in the City I've had a Swiss bank account and it's very much a rule of thumb that no questions are asked. I'll just drive down to Geneva and bank the money. So what about you lot?'

'If you remember Pete, I was going to be a lottery winner, and I was planning to move to Norfolk as soon as I can,' Mike answered.

'What about you two?'

'We are both going to go to Las Vegas on a golfing holiday with our wives. We'll just say we got lucky and shared our winnings. Neither of us wants to leave Devon, so we'll be extra careful. Don't you agree, Roger?' Dave asked.

'Absolutely, after all £2 million's not bad for an evening's work,' he said grinning and clipping Dave round the ear.

'Right well that's settled then. The next time we all see each other again will be at the Eddystone Lighthouse. Let's hope it stays really calm, and you two make doubly sure you're in position Tuesday, Wednesday or Thursday by one o'clock in the morning. If we see no signal, we'll clearly know that the mission will have been aborted for that night, and I'll be in touch, okay? Everything's understood? If you have any final questions now is your last chance so ask away,' Pete said.

However the team appeared happy, and after saying goodnight went off to their rooms. Pete had agreed to meet Dave at the Weymouth/Cherbourg ferry departure lounge that Saturday morning. A few days earlier Dave had remembered that one of his fishing friends had married a French girl, and was now living in Cherbourg. He had been in touch to organise a boat to take them out to the Sylvania on Sunday.

'It's strange, but none of us really knows that much, if anything, about you now and yet you're the leader,' Dave remarked, as they sat having a drink on the ferry to Cherbourg. 'I know you're a City man but why are you doing this job? It can't be just for the money.'

'You're sort of right Dave. It's a challenge, but also once I have my £4m I'm then made for life and will be comfortably off. And this is certainly a one-off. My nerves are pretty shredded already, and we've only just got going today!

Anyway, fancy another drink?'

'Yes, why not? Thanks.'

Dave's friend Len had booked them into a small hotel on the sea front in Cherbourg, and had agreed to meet for dinner to discuss Monday's trip. His wife was away visiting her parents, and so the three of them sat down for dinner.

'I'll pick you up very early tomorrow morning on the way to the harbour. Ideally, I want to get you on board without anyone noticing otherwise it's going to look a bit odd, my coming back alone. I have now got the Sylvania's midday position. Hopefully there will be no hiccups. By the way, you owe me 3000 euros for the pleasure.'

'Yes of course, sorry,' said Pete handing over an envelope, 'it's all there.'

'I believe you. If it isn't, you won't see me tomorrow that's for sure. I suggest you get an early night. I don't know what you are ultimately up to, but good luck anyway and thanks for the dinner. I'll see you at four o'clock tomorrow morning.' He got up, shook them both by the hand and left the restaurant.

'Probably rushed off to count the money, don't you think Pete?'

'Yes and I don't blame him. Come on, he's right; let's get an early night.'

'Hang on Pete. I'm only halfway through my cognac. Steady now.'

'You're right Dave. In fact I've now changed my mind. I'll join you and then get the bill.'

The following morning they were both up at 3.30 am, and ready outside the hotel, where Len picked them up half an hour later.

'That's my boat there. I've moved it as close as I can. The

cabin is open, so jump out now sharpish and get below and keep out of sight. I'll bring your bags.'

They did as they were told and Len waved at his old friend, Monsieur Dubois, who was on duty that morning, and steered his vessel out of the harbour into the Channel for their rendezvous with the Sylvania.

Once out of sight of Cherbourg, Pete and Dave were allowed on deck. It was a beautiful summer morning, with not a cloud in the sky and hardly any breeze at all.

'Well whatever you're up to you've certainly got the weather for it. I don't think I have ever seen so many stars as I did when I was driving home last night and the sea is like a millpond. The forecast for tonight is good, with clear skies and a full moon. We should spot the Sylvania sometime this afternoon. So make yourselves at home. One of you could boil up some water. I'm dying for a cuppa. My wife really doesn't know how to make proper dark brown, strong tea. It's funny it always tastes better on board. Off you go Dave. Very strong, dash of milk and two sugars - perfect.'

Later that afternoon the Sylvania came into view. She was actually quite a small cargo vessel which was going to make boarding that much easier.

'Thank God it's so calm. Getting people on board is not always easy. Get your rucksacks on, and be prepared to hit the rope ladder on my command. Great meeting you both, and good luck!'

Len's seamanship was excellent but even though the sea was calm, there was the inevitable swell as the two vessels came alongside. In the end they both got off easily and stood on the bridge of the Sylvania and waved goodbye to Len's fishing boat.

The Captain showed them their cramped quarters, and

then took them on deck and unlocked one of the holds on the deck.

'There is your RIB, one of the biggest, with all the drugs stashed on board. I can see why you need to make sure the coast is clear. Eddystone will be difficult to manoeuvre into but your man will have the moonlight, and also I understand, he was the keeper there once. In these conditions he should have no problem. I'll call you when we can just see Eddystone's beam, and then we'll quickly lower the RIB and you can be on your way. We'll then steam up the Channel as fast as possible, away from your operation.'

Back in Devon, the other part of the plan had gone smoothly. Pete had already texted them the okay to go ahead that night, due to the favourable weather conditions. They had parked the Volvo early on Monday morning, left their wet suits in the car, and had openly walked to Noss Mayo. They picked up the RIB, and to all intents and purposes went off on their planned lobster trip. Once the coast was clear, and their satellite communication device showed no activity around the lighthouse, they veered off course away from the lobster pots, to their destination - Eddystone.

Negotiating the rocks around the lighthouse was quite tricky, and to their delight, once they'd forced the lock they found it was not alarmed. Next, they pulled the RIB out of the water, and hid it in the bowels of the lighthouse.

'Now the fun starts,' said Mike, climbing up the steps inside the lighthouse. 'I've got nearly three hours to try and work out how to change from the double flash to a triple one, within a two minute window just after one o'clock.'

However, once Mike was in the control room, it all came flooding back, and he felt really confident for the first time that day.

'Roger, please open the manual at page 47, and hold it there for me so I can read the instructions.'

After a while Mike felt increasingly relaxed, as he easily manipulated the different lenses. After only half an hour he said:

'It's done. All I need to do is press that button there at one o'clock and we'll get triple, not double, flashes for exactly two minutes, as planned.'

This left them nearly a couple of hours waiting time, which dragged by very slowly. But it was far worse for Pete and Dave, not knowing how things were progressing at Eddystone..

Finally, at one o'clock, after a thorough sweep of the bay, and then round and out to sea making sure the coast was clear, Mike changed the beam to a triple flash to last just those two crucial minutes.

'There it is!' Pete cried out. Their RIB was quickly but carefully lowered from the Sylvania into the calm sea below - and they were off on full throttle.

Meanwhile, back on land, Bill unable to sleep, was sitting in his dressing gown watching the Eddystone lighthouse from his conservatory. One triple flash and then another, again and again, and then it went back to normal. Bill rubbed his eyes in disbelief, something was wrong. His "baby" was "out of tune" and that meant there was definitely something wrong.

Meanwhile Mike and Roger were nervously awaiting the arrival of their mates. They needn't have worried, as Pete and Dave arrived at top speed within the planned half an hour. As there was quite a swell, securing the RIB, with its full cargo to the rocks proved quite difficult. In the end the other two managed to clamber aboard. They were all very pumped up, and in all the excitement, they had all failed to think about checking around the back of the lighthouse over the last hour or so thinking that no-one could have approached it from the shore earlier. How wrong they were. They were sadly too over confident, and believed that all they had to do was leave the lighthouse, beach the RIB, move the heist to the car, get to London and do the deal later that morning with Pedro. They would soon be rich, after completing a job well done.

But as their RIB was about to cast off from the lighthouse rocks it was lit up by a hugely powerful beam of light, temporarily blinding them. It was Customs and Excise in one super-sized RIB, which had earlier been cleverly manouevered in behind the lighthouse and out of sight of Mike and Roger. Carelessly they had only been looking out to sea for the arrival of their mates.

'Our guns are trained on you. Put your hands above your heads. Come on! All of you! Don't try any tricks. You're all under arrest for breaking and entering the lighthouse, for a start. However,' the Officer shouted above the noise of the sea crashing onto the rocks, 'I think we'll find a few more things to charge you with by the looks of those thick plastic bags badly hidden and stashed away over there.' he said pointing to the stern.

'For Christ's sake! Who tipped you off?' shouted Mike furiously, as the Customs and Excise men boarded their RIB to arrest them.

'I did Mike, I'm afraid!' Bill cried out loudly so he could be heard above the roar of the waves, as the two RIBs were tossed about. 'I thought you were up to something the other day, when I saw you out with Charlie Wyvill, but I just couldn't work out what it was. So, that was an intriguing plan of yours to go for the triple flash, but you were careless, weren't you Mike? Surely you of all people must remember that I was her last keeper and lighthouse keepers are known insomniacs? It so happens that I was wide awake as usual, and was just admiring the view when I saw the first triple flash, and as it continued it was enough for me to call the Coastguards. You see, I instinctively knew that something was wrong.'

Bill then turned abruptly and pointed at the lighthouse and shouted loudly so everyone could hear him.

'I know all there is to know about this lighthouse. That's why the locals refer to Eddystone as "Bill's baby"!! Thank you Eddystone! You are indeed "my baby" and, as usual, you haven't let me down!'

A SMALL MATTER OF 7,200 SECONDS

Simon and Anna had been an item on and off for over four years. They both lived life to the full and consequently had the occasional disagreement about each other's nocturnal habits. Anna was prone to go on girls' nights until all hours, and although Simon was no saint, it did sometimes cause aggravation. It often resulted in a cooling-off period. However, "what the eye does not see" was their maxim. If their lifestyles were pretty volatile, they were never apart for more than a few days, except when following some sort of self-induced hiatus. They worked in the City and were both highly successful, each of them owning their own flat.

Simon was in his early thirties, and five years older than Anna. Both were attractive, and as their friends often said -"they made a lovely couple". An enchanted match you might suppose, but there was one aspect of their relationship that jarred. Simon hated skiing, whilst Anna, who had been a chalet girl in Klosters when she was eighteen, loved it and was a talented skier. Right at the beginning of their romance, she had persuaded him to join her party in Meribel. It had not been a success, so Anna went off skiing with her friends, but without Simon, for a week over New Year, a couple of weeks in February and the odd weekend if she could.

To begin with, Simon had not minded too much but, as the years went by, he became bored sitting at home knowing she was having a wonderful time. He did not have a black book of past girlfriends to contact and, anyway, everyone he knew seemed to be accounted for. He somewhat selfishly thought if Anna was having such a good time, why shouldn't he? He could just about justify this as Anna always came back banging on about how she had met this super guy who skied alone with her off-piste in the powder snow, and then they danced the night away and whatever. It was what was unsaid that irked him, although invariably after a week or two she came down to earth.

Now February had come round once again, and Anna was off to Aspen for a fortnight. Probably just as well, as for the first time in their relationship, they'd started bickering badly. It began at Christmas, while Simon was staying with Anna at her parents' house in Kent. He had played an appalling round of golf with Graham, Anna's father, and was therefore in a pretty crabby mood that evening at a local cocktail party. Anna knew everyone, and was particularly flirtatious with an attractive forty-year-old guy called Neil.

'Darling,' enthused Anna,'you simply must meet Neil. He's been working on the Brighton murder trial and it's all so interesting. As much as he can tell me, of course.'

Actually Simon and Neil got on very well which slightly irked Anna. On the way home she said:

'I couldn't get a word in edgeways. You monopolised him.'

'Well it was your suggestion that I met him, not mine,' Simon replied in a "yah boo sucks" tone of voice.

That's how it was for the next few weeks. There was always a niggle, with either one or the other taking the moral high ground, and the words "give and take" for once sadly missing from their joint vocabularies. The situation was not helped by the fact that Anna had moved in with Simon a week before she was due to leave to go skiing, as her flat was being redecorated. The close and constant proximity was causing quite a lot of grief. Simon was very minimalist and tidy. Anna was not. They say that opposites attract, but not at close quarters apparently.

'I've never appreciated how soulless your flat really is. I mean everything is so neat and tidy. It has no character. It could be one of those show flats on the Embankment.'

'Tough!' Simon replied. 'I like it, and you've never complained before, so what's the story?'

'Sorry. Perhaps I was a bit harsh. I suppose it's because I'm actually living here, rather than just spending the night. I'd rather have my flat any day. At least it's got some character.'

'Each to his own,' Simon retorted.

'You really don't like criticism do you, darling?' Anna said snidely. 'I've noticed that quite a lot recently. Maybe it's an age thing, and you're getting set in your ways. Never mind, I'm off tomorrow.'

"Thank God," thought Simon, wishing her away then and there. He was a bit annoyed he had offered to take her to Heathrow, as he was going to miss the England vs France international. At least he would know she had gone. That departure gate could not come soon enough for Simon. Despite the bickering they had a pleasant enough evening, and were due to leave for the airport late the following morning .

Saturday was frosty and clear and because Anna had gone back to her flat to sort out all her skiing gear, Simon picked her up at midday. The drive out to the airport was uneventful with little to say that wasn't inane. Things like :

'This time tomorrow you'll be up some God-awful mountain with a hunk of a man bashing the piste.'

'What about you? Tonight, in your dreams, you'll be shacked up in a bar with a leggy blonde downing a few martinis, and desperately trying to make the right impression!'

'You're right. In my dreams,' Simon replied churlishly.

Prior to checking in Anna had agreed to meet the rest of her party at the bar in Terminal 5 at Heathrow. True to form there they were all there. Loud and brash as ever, well into the holiday spirit.

'Hi Anna. Hi Simon,' they all whinnied at once. 'Glass of shampoo?' Simon cringed, and was reminded of the other reason he did not rate skiing, it was Anna's skiing friends. He could not cope with their endless braying, and skiing stories throughout the year. To be fair, he got on well with her other friends. It was just this lot - the Dirty Dozen they called themselves. However, he did have a soft spot for one of them called Marina. She never seemed to have a boyfriend, and always latched onto Simon when the "Dozen" were around.

'Hi Marina!' Simon enthused, 'you're looking lovelier than ever. '

'And you too,' Marina replied, moving Simon away from the group. 'I've got something to tell you. I've met a really nice guy at last, called Rob. I nearly didn't come on this trip, but I'd booked, so here I am.'

'Tell me all.' It was quite a story so they had a good laugh together.

'What about you and Anna? It must be about five years

now isn't it?'

'Yeah. It is. You make it sound like a life sentence,' Simon replied dejectedly.

'Personally, and I'm sorry to say this, surely your relationship must have run its course by now?' Marina said in a strange way.

'Yeah. It hasn't been great since Christmas. But now you're not available,' Simon joked, 'what can I do?'

'Oh, shut up! You've never fancied me. Just good friends, Marina and Simon. But I'll tell you what. Go out there when we're away and get yourself laid. You need a change. Listen to your Auntie Marina,' she said giggling and eyeballing Simon. 'If you do, please report back!'

'Chance would be a fine thing,' Simon said. 'Anyway, I'm out of practice.'

'Excuses, excuses. Go for it Simon. Enjoy life before it's too late.'

'What are you two up to?' asked Anna, ostentatiously draping herself around Simon, as if she totally owned him.

'Nothing much Anna. I just told him he ought to get laid when you were away,' Marina replied cheekily.

'He's too exhausted and faithful. Aren't you darling?' Anna said.

'You make him sound like a smelly old labrador,' Marina said, laughing.

'He is! Aren't you my sweetheart?

Simon cringed and was more than happy when it was time for them to check in. After much good-byeing and kissing, the Dirty Dozen eventually went through to the security gate. Simon felt strangely elated and was just setting off for the car park when someone tapped him on his shoulder. Turning round, he could not believe his eyes.

Standing there before him was a woman of such beauty that he thought he must be on a film set, and this was the leading lady. She was Ingrid Bergman, Julie Christie and Sienna Miller rolled into one.

'Sorry to bother you, and you probably don't remember me. I'm Rebecca, Charles Davenport's younger sister. I've just come back from Antigua, saw you and thought. "He just might be able to give me a lift back into town". Is that a bit cheeky? I did wait until all your friends had left. Is the tall blonde-haired one your girlfriend? She's very pretty. Sorry, I'm talking too much. Your turn.' Her green eyes sparkled and she smiled at Simon, a smile he rather liked.

'No, sorry, I mean yes. I'm afraid I'm a little confused.. You caught me by surprise. Do I know Charles Davenport?'

'Of course you do. You were both at school together and I was the kid sister who used to turn up and embarrass him,' she replied.

'Excellent. Yes, now I do remember. But how you've grown. I mean, um... sorry, grown up!'

'Heavens above. I should hope so. I'm all of twenty- four now. Single and with a sort of proper job as well. I run the lunch time trade in a restaurant off the King's Road called The Peach Tree. Do you know it?' she asked walking close to Simon who had somehow, in amongst the banter, offered to carry her suitcase.

'Yes and yes. I know The Peach Tree - excellent place. Now if you can keep up with me, I'll give you a lift to town.'

Rebecca did a little jig, kissed Simon lightly on the cheek and said

'You're a star. I've had such a terrible holiday in Antigua. I'll tell you all about it in the car.'

Despite the fact that Rebecca seemed to be more of

a chatter-trunk than a chatter-box, he was enjoying her impulsive character and apparent cheerfulness despite the ruined holiday. On the way back he was given chapter and verse which, strangely, he did not mind one bit. Rebecca was such a vibrant and engaging person that he loved listening to her. Occasionally he glanced round towards her, to check out her immense and seemingly natural beauty. In fact he was enjoying himself so much that he drove as slowly as he dared to stay in her company for as long as he could.

Her life seemed horribly complicated, separated parents rowing constantly through their lawyers, a schmuck of a boyfriend who had ditched her in Antigua and gone off on a yacht with another girl to do the Antigua to Cape Town Race, and this was only on day two.

Fortunately, she had been befriended by a couple in their mid-fifties who she had met in Admiral's Harbour, and they offered her a bunk on their yacht. That bit had been good fun in the end.

'Now you can see nothing much has gone right for me over the last fortnight. To cap it all, I've got nowhere to live for the next couple of weeks, as the completion date on my new flat has been delayed. I've been offered the odd sofa but I'm a bit old for all that. Know anybody who might be able to put me up? I'd pay, of course.'

As it happened, Simon did. A great friend of his, Nigel Atkinson, had recently divorced, but part of the deal was that he kept the marital home, whilst his "ex" pocketed a fortune. He was always on the look out for lodgers. But Simon had another idea.

'Look, Rebecca. I know this might seem a bit forward, but how about moving into my place until Anna comes back?' he asked, holding her bemused gaze as they stopped at a red light.

'Oh wow, that would be fantastic! Won't Anna kick up a stink when she comes back?'

'I can handle Anna. Anyway, she doesn't actually live with me. She has her own place and frankly she doesn't need to know,' he said pulling away slowly from the lights.

'Excellent. I'd love to. Can we stop off at my sister's place, so I can pick up the gear I need. Sorry, I never asked, where do you live?'

'Wandsworth. Off Earlsfield Road.'

'Couldn't be better. My sister's house is in The Tonsleys. This is all so exciting. Two weeks with a virtual stranger who I always had a schoolgirl crush on. What's the rent?' she asked forcefully. 'I must pay, otherwise I'll feel like a kept woman. Actually that sounds rather fun!'

'No rent. The deal is you take me out to dinner a couple of times and The Peach Tree doesn't count,' Simon said, laughing and catching her eyes, which seemed to him to be dancing. "Oh my God," he thought, "what am I up to? Still it could be a lot of fun!"

And it was. After picking up some of Rebecca's gear from her sister, they unloaded it and went straight to his local, The Alma, at her suggestion. Simon respected her immediately. A few drinks in his local was just what he needed. He proudly introduced Rebecca to his mates as his friend's younger sister and they returned to his flat in the best of moods.

And so it was that the days flew by. Rebecca loved Simon's flat and said all the right things about minimalism. Simon's work colleagues and friends could not believe the difference.

'How is it that with Anna being away, you're on such

good form, Simon?' he kept being asked. It would have been easy easy for Simon to answer, but he didn't. Rebecca was his secret, and that's the way it was to be. They kept themselves to themselves. Rebecca kept her side of the bargain and took Simon out to dinner three times in all. Simon, ever the perfect gentleman, reciprocated a couple of times. So they wined and dined but also spent quiet evenings in the flat just talking, mainly about Simon and his on-off relationship with Anna, rather than Rebecca's recent short-lived romance.

The more they talked, the more Simon realised his life was speeding by, and that he had not been happy, really happy, for the past year. He definitely needed a break, and Rebecca was proving to be the catalyst. He realised by the second week, although he had made no advances, that he might be falling in love and that whatever happened between Rebecca and himself, he wanted to finish with Anna. As much as anything to restore his sanity, but also to be a free spirit again.

'Simon, I've had such fun being with you,' Rebecca said late one night, curled up on the sofa sipping a glass of whisky. You're so like my brother who has always been my bestest friend. I've been really happy and relaxed in your flat and with you. I'll miss it so much, although I've got plenty to do to my place once I leave here. Actually, that must be quite soon mustn't it?'

'Yes, Anna's back the day after tomorrow - Sunday. I'm afraid you'll have to leave that morning,' Simon said sadly, drinking long and hard on his whisky.

'Don't sound so miserable. Remember what we agreed. "Friends are friends forever."We can still see each other can't we?'

'Yes, of course we will. We will.' If only, thought Simon, if only as more than just friends. Time will tell, he mused.

On their last night together they celebrated in some style, and in the taxi on the way home, Rebecca held Simon's hand and rested her head on his shoulder.

' "Bliss was it in that dawn to be alive, " ' quoted Simon.

'"But to be young was very heaven." Wordsworth.' Rebecca replied, cuddling up to him. When they got back to the flat they both curled up on the sofa to have their whisky nightcap.

'Before we drink far too much I have a proposition for you.'

'The short answer is, thank you and the longer one, not at the moment. I need time to think about it,' Rebecca said, laughing uncontrollably and enjoying Simon's embarrassment.

'No! No! No! Rebecca you stupid old thing.I didn't mean it that way.'

'Don't worry Simon. Why, we hardly know each other and certainly not in the biblical sense! Yet,' she said cheekily.

'Please, Rebecca, hear me out,' Simon said quite seriously.

'OK. Sorry. Fire away.'

Simon took Rebecca into his confidence and explained what was needed. After a while, Rebecca swallowed the last of her whisky, got up and gave Simon a kiss on his forehead, tousled his hair playfully and said.

'I'll make up my mind during the night and let you know in the morning. Sweet dreams!'

'But the morning might be too late,' Simon shouted at her.

'We'll see,' and she closed the door of her room.

Anna had texted to say she was getting a lift in from Heathrow the following morning, but Simon had no idea exactly when. He tossed and turned trying to get to sleep, worrying how Rebecca had taken his proposition. Just as he was at last falling asleep he felt a light tap on his shoulder. It was Rebecca, softly lit by the hall light shining into his bedroom. She looked gorgeous in a pair of his old pyjamas. He sat up, as she sat on his bed.

'I said I'd tell you in the morning.'

'But it's late, well past two o'clock.'

'So what? It's morning, and the answer is yes and no, on one condition,' she said getting up to close his bedroom door. 'It should be fairly obvious now,' she said as she slipped out of his pyjamas and got under the duvet. 'Just this once, darling Simon, and then we go our separate ways. I've waited and waited for you this past fortnight but you've always been such a gentleman and you'll always be my friend.'

'Ssh... Rebecca,' Simon said as he took her in his arms holding her close to him and seeking her mouth, her tongue, her everything.

At 10 o'clock that morning they were both woken by the phone. It was Anna.

'Wonderful holiday, darling. I'm just dropping off my stuff at my flat and then I'll come straight round. Tell you all about it, sweetie, when I see you.'

Rebecca started to get out of his bed.

'No, no stay please. This will make everything so much more realistic.'

'Are you sure Simon? Isn't it a bit cruel? Let's do it the way we discussed.'

'OK. You're probably right,' he replied. 'I'll get us some breakfast. Just plonk yourself on the sofa in my old towelling dressing gown. Show a lot of leg and look sexy.

Not a problem in your case.'

'Cheeky!' But she did as had been planned.

Anna arrived within half an hour and in she came, larger than life.

'Darling, I've had such a wonderful time. Excuse me but what exactly is going on here? Who on earth is this strange person?'

'I'm not a person. I'm Rebecca, and I've been staying with Simon for a couple of weeks waiting for the completion on my flat.'

'Completion, my foot!' Anna replied angrily, her voice rising by the second. 'What's the meaning of this Simon? The minute my back is turned you bring in some floosie! Well, I've had it with you big time!'

'Anna, please let me - '

'Don't try and wriggle out of this one Simon. My God have I been a fool or what?. I should have....'

'It isn't how it looks Anna.'

'No? It is to me! What a bastard you've turned out to be! That's it Simon. Finished. Finito. You can keep your floosie.'

'But! But! Hear me out.'

'No way. Goodbye. Arriverderci. Adios and Au Fucking Revoir! You sad and sick nobody! And the same to you, you fucked-up floosie,' she yelled, marching out of the flat and slamming the door hard.

'It worked like a dream Rebecca, thank you so much,' Simon enthused.

'Wow! She's something else. I must get packed and be off. Can you get me a taxi?'

'Okay I will. But that's it is it?' he asked forlornly.

'Of course it is. We made a pact,' she said smiling. 'And the answer to your second proposition is "no", for at least six months, until we're both sorted. You've had baggage and so have I. So please - six months from today. No calls. No contact. No nothing until then.'

'It's a huge gamble.'

'So, gamble away. It's only one hundred and eighty two and a half days,' she said laughing and getting her gear together.

'Just wait. Let me get my brain round this. It's four thousand, three hundred and eighty hours, roughly,' he said sadly. 'How on earth can I wait that long?'

'Put like that it seems a lifetime' she replied, 'the doorbell, my taxi. Thanks for everything Simon. You've been more than great,' she said flinging her arms around him and stifling a tear. 'I'm the cool one. Gulp. I must go. Ciao, etc. darling,' and she fled awkwardly down the stairs with all her various bits of paraphernalia.

The taxi driver had seen it all before as he looked at Rebecca in his mirror, sobbing away quietly in the back of his cab and telling him everything that had just happened.

'I can cope with,' sniffle, sniffle, sob, sob, 'over a hundred and eighty days, but four thousand and three hundred and eighty something hours. I just don't know. '

'Tell you what, miss. Go back to your flat. Unpack. Have a bath. Change into your favourite jeans and top, sit down and think about it. Here's my card. Call me if you want and we could make a grand entrance together.'

'Excellent. Thanks. I will'

And she did. Seven thousand and two hundred seconds later, with her cabby friend Joe, Rebecca was standing outside Simon's flat. She rang the buzzer, holding Joe's hand very tightly to boost her confidence.

'Hi, Simon. Hi, Simon,' she repeated nervously, 'it's me

Rebecca. I could cope with the days, but not the hours, minutes and particularly the seconds.'

'Stay there. Don't move,' he said as he locked up his flat, rushed downstairs and into the street. All he saw was Rebecca, and he rushed into her arms, kissing her all over as she was trying to contain her tears.

'What we need now is a taxi to take us to the Ritz or the Berkeley or the Dorchester for champagne and caviar.

'No problem, sir. Rebecca and I are old friends. Aren't we luv?' said Joe emerging from the shadows. 'My carriage awaits. There's no charge. But it'd better be the Berkeley I think. It's the nearest and we'll be there in a matter of minutes.'

'Make it seconds,' they both replied happily, as they hopped into his cab.

BUSINESS AND PLEASURE

'Good morning Jane. And how are you this lovely spring-like day?' Ben asked his PA as he rushed past her into his office, late as usual.

'Fine thank you, Ben. I've just had a rather weird phone call from a friend of a friend of yours called Marcus O'Leary. I've left the number on your desk. Wasn't he that mad Irish billionaire who started up a mobile phone company in Ireland called Eireophone a few years back?'

'You're quite right, and I've got a feeling his advertising account is up for grabs. So please do me a print-out from his website, and I'll give him a call.'

Ben ran a highly successful, but relatively small, creative advertising agency called Protocol. He, and his business partner, Henry, had built it up in the early nineties into one of London's most creative outfits. Just as he was finishing his coffee, his phone rang, and Jane put him through to an old university friend of his, who he hadn't seen for far too long.

Rob how are you? Where are you and what are you up to?' Ben enquired.

'Ben it's been far too long. I can't really chat now, but have you just had a call from Marcus O'Leary? It's just that...' and he carried on.

Ben idly gazed out of his window at a very attractive woman getting out of her Mercedes parked in Glebe Place, just off the King's Road, obviously intent on some serious retail therapy. "Another day in paradise" for her, he thought.

'Sorry Rob. I missed most of that. Slight hangover.'

'Ben, please get a grip. I said I needed to see you right away. It's about O'Leary's daughter, his advertising account and a game of golf. I really can't talk now, but you're having lunch with me at Bluebird at one o'clock today. Your secretary has just booked it. She told me you were free. Please don't be late, it's important.'

Ben had no idea what was going on. He had been great chums with Rob at Cambridge, although over the last few years they'd drifted apart. From their brief conversation it sounded to him that Rob wasn't married, and that something was up between him and O'Leary's daughter. But where did the game of golf fit in? He was intrigued, and was looking forward to lunch, hoping all would be revealed.

Ben was in his late thirties, married with two children, and commuted from his home in Sussex. He was tall and athletic looking and, while business was important, he liked nothing better than being at home with his family. That was if he wasn't playing golf. He'd got his Blue at Cambridge, and for a while played in a number of Amateur events, and when selected, went to Rye each year for the President's Putter. But now he had a family there was less time for golf, though whenever he could he would fix up a game at his club, West Sussex, where he'd been a member for twenty years. He certainly knew the course well after all that time, and still had to a low handicap.

Jane came into the office and handed Ben the print-out of Eireophone's website.

'Shall I get Mr O'Leary on the phone for you Ben?' she asked.

'No thanks. Could you call him to say I'm in a meeting until four o'clock and then you can call him? As you know I'm having lunch with Rob and he can fill me in before I get to talk to our billionaire friend. After all, if their account is on the move, the more I know about him and his business the better.'

Protocol to some outsiders seemed a trifle arrogant, as the agency never did any speculative pitches for potential clients. It was felt that their outstanding work on past and current campaigns spoke for itself. Their staggering growth over the last five years endorsed this new business strategy, so Ben was quite excited at the prospect of talking to Marcus O'Leary. Hopefully it would be about business but also it would appear to be about his daughter and Rob and, of course, golf.

The morning couldn't go quickly enough for Ben who had endless focus group reports to wade through, and the inevitable creative tantrums. He spoke to Henry, his partner and creative director, about O'Leary, and they agreed to have a drink after work to give it all some more thought.

Bluebird is one of Conran's better enterprises, and the more senior staff at Protocol tended to use it as their canteen. They could afford to. Ben saw Rob sitting at a table by the window, walked up to him and shook his hand warmly and said,

'How long's it been? You look well and fit.'

'At least five years. And yes I do feel great, it must be love! I think we last met at old Johnnie Thomson's wedding down in Gloucestershire. Do you remember? You'd just had your first child and I'd just lost the one love of my life and was still looking. This is why I need to talk to you about old man O'Leary and his daughter Clare, and golf of course!'

'The plot thickens and I'm all ears. A glass of champagne first perhaps?'

'Good idea. Waiter - two glasses of champagne please. Let me fill you in. After Sarah gave me the boot I was a tragic and forlorn figure and really didn't socialise at all for quite a long time. And then I met Clare at a dinner party a few months ago.'

He explained the meeting in some detail, and how in love he was with her and she with him. It all sounded great to Ben, and he seemed to be just the same energetic and lovable rogue he'd known at Cambridge. It was good to see him again, and Ben was waiting anxiously for the denouement or put more simply, why this free lunch totally out of the blue?

'I have a problem,' Rob said wearily.

'Let me guess,' Ben said, 'old man O'Leary and Clare's, his only daughter.'

'Absolutely spot on.'

'But where does the game of golf fit in?'

'Let me explain. It's really quite simple. I'm in love with his daughter and I've just proposed to her but her father has yet to agree to our union as it were. He's not particularly enamoured with me for two fundamental reasons. Firstly I'm not Roman Catholic, and secondly I don't play golf!'

'You could always convert,' Ben said smiling, 'but where does the golf bit fit in? Don't tell me his daughter plays off scratch,' Ben was now laughing loudly.

'Ben. Please. It's not a laughing matter!'

'Sorry, Rob. That would have been the case in a PG Wodehouse story. But of course this is fact not fiction. So how do I fit into this intrigue?'

'It's the small matter of golf. I'm sure I can talk O'Leary round on the religious side but it's the golf that's the stumbling block. He is a complete addict. If it's not his highly successful mobile phone business, it's his golf. Wherever he plays he spends a fortune in the Professional's shop trying to find some piece of elusive equipment to cure his slice, his hook or whatever. Apparently, according to Clare, he's got any number of different sets of clubs and at least a dozen different putters. He's forever changing his balls, sounds rather painful, and thinks nothing of buying armfuls of gadgets to improve his game. From luminous golf balls to special golf gloves, massive umbrellas, and even an electronic range finder which works rather like a pair of binoculars. To cap it all, he's just built a driving range and practice green at his new pile of bricks in Sussex. I'm convinced he's keeping the golf companies solvent, and I'm also convinced there will soon be a major golfing company called O'Leary. So you see he's a complete fanatic, and has a deep respect for the game, its rules and traditions.'

Ben still could not quite work out what his role was going to be in the matter of O'Leary and his golf.

All was revealed as Rob continued.

'I was staying with Clare's father, when would you believe it, your name cropped up?'

'Why on earth?'

'Well. They now live very near Pulborough and he's actually just become a member of your golf club. You're obviously still a good player as he'd seen your name up on most of the Winners' boards and he wanted to know if you were the same Hobson who ran Protocol. And once he'd found that out, he mentioned it to me over lunch on Sunday and I said that you and I had been friends at

Cambridge. And, do you know, for the first time since I've met him he actually smiled at me and said, "Well you can't be all bad Rob. How well did you know him?" So of course I explained, and said we hadn't seen each other for a while but that we'd always been good friends.'

"Excellent," he'd replied, "excellent. We could have some fun here. You never know if you ask me I may yet happily agree to you marrying Clare, but for the moment my answer is; wait for a while until I've sorted out a little plan".

'So what's it all about then?' Ben asked quizzically.

'Ben. I've no idea except that you're obviously the key. Presumably he'll tell you this afternoon but for God's sake don't say you've had lunch with me. Keep me out of the equation for the moment, but please let me know what's going on.'

As Ben left Bluebird he thought to himself that the plot wasn't just thickening, it had thickened. He'd taken Rob's mobile number, and promised to report back as soon as he could.

When the call came promptly at four o'clock, rather than O'Leary talking to Ben it was his PA fixing a lunch date for Friday that week apparently for - "business and pleasure".

Both Ben and Rob were mystified, but all they could do was try and wait until the end of the week. Ben met up with Henry, his business partner, after work for a drink at The Phoenix as arranged. Henry couldn't make head or tail of it although he felt optimistic on the "business" side. Eireophone would be a massive coup for Protocol, so he advised Ben to go fully prepared on the UK mobile phone market.

'No probs. I'll get one of our planners to brief me fully.'

And so the days dragged by until his luncheon date

at O'Leary's club, The Carlton. Ben was beginning to understand the vagaries of the mobile phone market and now kept noticing Eireophone's advertising, and was not impressed. Not surprising that the account was on the move. Poor Rob and Clare couldn't stand the strain, so Ben and his wife Georgie took them out to dinner at Caraffini in Chelsea. They both agreed that Rob and Clare made a great couple, although none of them could understand what O'Leary was up to.

'But surely Clare you must have some idea of what this is all about?'

'No. I just can't work it out,' she replied, 'although it must have something to do with golf, and the fact that he's now a member of your club, Ben. I expected Dad to turn down Rob's proposal to me on religious grounds but he actually gave no reason - just said, wait as he now had a plan. This was after Rob said he knew you Ben. To be quite honest I thought that Dad would insist Rob took up golf, and give him six months to learn and then get him to challenge him for my hand. That could have been quite fun, don't you think darling?' she said smiling at Rob, who paled visibly. He'd certainly never been much of a sportsman at Cambridge. Bright but not sporty.

Clare, who had gorgeous, jet black hair and a ready smile, patted Rob on the hand and said,

'Cheer up darling. Now that I've met your friend Ben I'm sure that he'll be a good match for my father. When it comes to business my Dad's a cool cookie, but with golf, if someone can give him advice that works, he'll be a friend for life. So over to you Ben! Oh and one last thing before I forget. Don't be late and don't be early. You must arrive dead on time. It's one of his foibles. If he says one o'clock for lunch and to meet him in the bar, then it has to be one o'clock sharp. I think that's the main reason he fired one of his last agencies - poor time keeping.'

It was agreed that Ben would meet Clare and Rob for an early drink at The Surprise, after meeting O'Leary, so he could fill them in before he went to Sussex for the weekend.

There was no way Ben was going to be early or late, so he arrived in the main bar at The Carlton at exactly one o'clock, Friday afternoon. Marcus O'Leary was a well-known figure. Ben recognised him at once and went up and introduced himself.

'Mmm - not bad. Only ten seconds late by my watch. I like people to be on time, but I'm sure you've been well briefed by my daughter and Rob, and don't tell me you haven't seen them. What will you have? Bill here makes a mean Martini.'

'That would be great,' Ben replied noticing that in the flesh Marcus was a fit and lean man of sixtyish with clear, blue twinkling eyes. He looked interesting, and Ben was looking forward to hearing what he had to say.

'As my PA said on the phone, Ben, this is business and pleasure both inextricably linked but, be warned, I never talk business over lunch. Why ruin good food? We'll wait until later when we have coffee and liqueurs in the lounge. For the moment tell me all about your good self and I'll bring you up to speed on the O'Leary family.'

And so that's the way it was, with Ben very much taking the lead as Marcus was particularly keen to hear about his golf at Cambridge and his early Amateur tournaments.

'Your daughter told me that you are a bit of a golf fanatic,' Ben said, drinking an excellent claret that had been ordered to go with their roast pheasant.

'That's an understatement dear boy. I'm completely mad

about golf. When I was a lad my father used to take me to Killarney to caddy for him. Those were almost the days of hickory shafts. I became hooked on the game, pardon the pun, but he wouldn't let me play at his course until I got down to a ten handicap, which I did by the time I was sixteen. Even then I had to play with second-hand equipment, and I vowed that once I'd made my fortune only the best would do which is why I've amassed rather a lot of golf equipment,' he said laughing, and pouring Ben another glass.

'It's really only been in the last ten years since Eireophone has taken off that I've been able to satisfy my whims on the golfing front. It really infuriates my wife, Siobhan. The garage at my new house in Sussex is where I hoard anything in golf that might improve my game. Wait 'til I tell you about my first set of made-to-measure Pings. You see it was only like this...'

And for the next three-quarter's of an hour, Marcus went through his entire collection of golfing equipment from Taylor Made to Callaway, Titleist to Nike, Pringle to Glenmuir, Odyssey to Ping Putters, Footjoy to Stylo and then back again through many more golf manufacturers and assorted gadgets. He claimed his favourite was his recent acquisition of a flashing golf ball, which flashed a maximum of two minutes once you'd hit it, but he wasn't able to find anyone interested in playing with him at night. As promised, business was not discussed over lunch, and as they moved into the club's drawing room Ben was looking forward to the business side. He'd grown to like this man and hoped the feeling was mutual. Eireophone in Protocol's client portfolio would indeed be quite a coup.

'Now young man,' Marcus said as he settled himself into

a comfortable, worn, leather armchair, 'down to business. You must be wondering what you're doing here listening to the ramblings of an old man wrapped up in his golf. I'm not actually a betting man and, despite being Irish, never have been. But I do like a challenge and this is where you come in. As you know Eireophone has been phenomenally successful in the UK, and it has made me a rich man. But frankly, I'm bored with my current advertising agency, whose work certainly helped our growth but whose efficiency and particularly timekeeping is poor. I'm a stickler for punctuality in business and, as far as golf is concerned, knowing the rules of the game and adhering to them implicitly. I admire Protocol and the work you've done recently. I also admire your single minded stance of refusing to do speculative pitches. You seem to attract blue-chip clients, so your strategy obviously works, and I'd like to do business with you. But there is a caveat. Let's turn to my daughter and her relationship with Rob. This is the pleasurable bit of the "business and pleasure", although I think it causes me more headaches than running my business. Anyway, hear me out.'

He then went on to say that Rob was basically a good guy, an extremely successful lawyer and despite the religious differences eminently suitable for his daughter, Clare. Although he'd never said this to anyone except Siobhan and now Ben, the one thing that upset him more than anything else was that Rob didn't play golf. He'd always envisaged a prospective son-in-law playing against him for his daughter's hand. It would be unique he thought, and well worth the punt. Rob was the first and only man Clare had fallen for and now she wanted to marry him and sadly he didn't play golf.

'You can see my dilemma. I'm a silly old thing really. I've always had this idea of a suitor playing golf against me for my daughter's hand. It's not as if Rob plays tennis or anything, but I have to confess I do like him and I think he'll make an excellent son-in-law. But I won't be denied my ambition of someone playing for my daughter's hand. This is where you come in. As you know I've just joined West Sussex Golf Club and apparently you are one of the best amateur members there. I do know that you are now off five, but this adds a certain frisson to my proposition - as that's also my handicap.'

What he then proposed left Ben aghast.

'My proposition is very simple. We play matchplay over eighteen holes at West Sussex. If you win you get my business and my blessing for Clare's marriage to Rob. If we half the match we go to extra holes until a winner is decided. If you lose, my business goes to JWT. Clare and Rob can of course still get married but without my blessing and some of her inheritance will go into building a 36-hole course near Dublin to be called The O'Leary Club. It's a big ask isn't it? Are you up to it? Oh, a couple of other things. Turn up exactly five minutes before we are due to tee off, take no longer than two minutes to play each shot and no more than five looking for your ball, which I'm sure will not happen anyway. That's one thing. The other is the R&A Rules of Golf. I'm always amazed how few people really know and understand them but I expect you do. We'll stick to them rigidly. Understood? And I will not allow you to ask my chauffeur caddy Seamus for any rulings. Understood?'

'Fine, but frankly Marcus I'm a bit overwhelmed. Why me and why now?' said Ben.

'It's obvious young man. For me you're in the right place

at the right time. I want your agency to handle my business, and I want to fulfil a whim I've had for many years over the matter of giving my approval to my daughter's choice of husband. For Rob read Ben. Simply put you are representing him and yourself, and fulfilling one of my lifetime's strange ambitions. I've discussed it with Siobhan and she's game, but Clare knows nothing about it. But please free to fill them in. What do you say?'

'I suppose I'm flattered on the business front and for that I thank you, but you've put some pressure on me on Clare and Rob's behalf. Still I did win the Amateur Championship once, and there was certainly pressure there when we got to the fifth extra hole and I holed a monster putt. However after that I didn't do so well in the Open Championship, missing the cut by at least six strokes. Never mind all that, I'm definitely on, but let me first clear it with your daughter. She may have other ideas.'

'Fine. If she agrees let's say the first Sunday afternoon in June, teeing off at four o'clock sharp, Mum's the word. No one else must know except for the obvious protagonists, including your business partner. I will bring Seamus my chauffeur as caddy and he's been busy measuring the course off the back tees. You may also, of course, bring a caddy if you choose.'

'No way thanks. Golf's difficult enough without somebody under or over clubbing you and tut-tutting round the course.' Actually Ben had in mind the Professional at West Sussex, Tim Packham, but wasn't going to mention it at this stage.

'Okay,' said Marcus getting up from his chair, and shaking Ben by the hand, 'may the best man win. See you on June the third.'

'Absolutely Marcus.' Ben wondered, as he was leaving the Carlton, which of the many sets of clubs Marcus would use on the day. He chuckled, thinking it could be fun, although Henry, Clare and Rob might not be quite so amused.

Henry couldn't believe his story when he told him back at the office later that afternoon. Clare and Rob were less incredulous.

'Actually it doesn't surprise me that much,' Clare said, sipping a glass of cold Bollinger at The Ivy. 'He's always been mad about his golf and the few men I've taken home have always been asked the same question, "What's your handicap?", which is why I've never wanted to go out with a golfer. And now at least we know where we stand although there's a bit of pressure on you to deliver Ben. If you win you'll be our best man in more than one way,' she said giggling nervously.

'But, Ben, do you think you're up to it? You really don't have to do it on our account, I'm sure he'll mellow,' said Rob.

'Ah! But that's the beauty of it. He knows I won't back out even if you wanted me to. Don't forget Eireophone is a £20 million piece of business. He's clever, he's got us on both accounts, as he so succinctly put it - "business and pleasure". Actually Clare, how good was he when he was younger?'

'Well I know he played off scratch, and he's won quite a few cups. It's his caddy Seamus you've got to watch. He used to caddy for one of the Irish professionals on the European Tour, and he's very cunning. He literally hands over the club he thinks my father should use, and as the expression goes he just "bangs the ball down the fairway and onto the green". I know he's only been a member at

West Sussex for a couple of months, but he tells me he's already broken par twice, whatever that means. He certainly seemed pretty pleased.'

'He would be,' Ben replied, 'that's no mean feat there. I certainly haven't done that in the last year or two. Still there's time yet. We've got eight weeks, and I'll make sure I get out on the course as much as possible. Having said I wouldn't have a caddy, I might ask Tim Packham, the Pro at West Sussex, to carry my bag. It would sort of mean we're playing level from the start. If anyone knows the course well, all about my game and importantly the rules of golf, Tim does. I'll call him tomorrow.'

Over the following eight weeks the two gladiators were out at different times on the course. The match had been kept secret, particularly as some club members might have thought it "poor form". It also allowed Marcus and Ben to go about their business. However, it did get back, via Clare that her father's golf was improving while the same could not be said about Ben's. Normally a very relaxed and phlegmatic player he now found his nerves playing him up, with his putting being a particular problem. The yips were something he'd never experienced before.

Tim took him aside one afternoon as Ben had been way over his handicap and seemed very down.

'Your main problem Ben is clearly your putting. Now tomorrow I want you up here at eight o'clock and we'll go onto the practice green with a selection of putters. I'm convinced you need a change and once you've found one that suits your style, stick with it. In my experience putting is all in the mind. If you find the right putter you'll be mentally sound and your touch will come back. I know you've had that putter for years but it's letting you down badly, just when you need all the confidence you can get. See you tomorrow. Sweet dreams.'

But sleep was one thing Ben couldn't get. Georgie and the children even complained that gentle Ben was getting irritable and losing his sense of humour. They were right of course, he was finding the whole thing a tremendous strain with so much at stake. In his amateur days he had played for his pride and the winning of a nice silver cup or two. But now the prize would be a huge business prospect and a marriage. He tossed and turned so much that night that Georgie suggested, in no uncertain manner, that the spare room might be the answer, where he at last got to sleep but overslept, and nearly missed his appointment with Tim.

What he didn't miss, however, was the hole. Tim had been right. One putter, a Scotty Cameron, suddenly gave Ben the confidence he needed, and he holed putt after putt after putt, from twenty feet to two feet. But even better he later took this new confidence out on the course and went round in level par.

'Well played Ben,' said Tim shaking his hand on the eighteenth, 'level par, only twenty four putts and you beat me by a stroke. That's much more like it. I'm beginning to look forward to caddying for you in a fortnight's time, if you can keep your game on song, I think you can do it.'

Finally the day of the match arrived. And what a beautiful day it was - a clear blue sky with not a breath of wind.

Ben had slept well and was really feeling up for it. Georgie had decided to come along and give him moral support, and had also asked Rob and Clare to spend the weekend with them. Saturday night dinner had been a sombre affair, with Rob being the most nervous and apprehensive of them all.

'I just feel so helpless not being able to contribute anything

Ben. And the whole thing is so finite it doesn't bear thinking about,' Rob moaned.

'Please, please, Rob. Stress less. I'm just going to treat it as another golf match. Important, yes, but a game nevertheless. We'll just have to see how it goes. But whatever happens let me assure you I've also got a lot riding on it, so I'll be trying my hardest. Just one word of advice. Walk round with us by all means, clap the good shots, but I'd rather you didn't talk to me at all. I prefer it that way as it helps my concentration. Tim and I will obviously work out yardages, club selection, and read the greens together. So cheer up Rob, it could be fun. We were thinking of having a referee, but it's been agreed that both our caddies know the rules of golf backwards. I'm pretty certain Marcus will question one or two rulings, as indeed I may.'

Promptly at 3.55pm Marcus, Seamus and Siobhan were joined on the first tee by Ben, Rob, Clare, Georgie and Ben's caddy, Tim.

Marcus was in a jovial mood and called heads as Ben tossed the coin. Heads it was and Marcus elected to drive off first. Now the first hole at West Sussex is a relatively easy par five and both players bisected the fairway with their drives, with Marcus slightly longer off the tee.

'What do you think Tim?' Ben asked.

'I'd play your five iron straight into the green, and go for a birdie to put the pressure on Marcus.'

Tim gave him the club, Ben settled over the ball and with his silky swing hit the ball high and long to the hole. But he'd pulled it slightly to the left, and the ball just missed the green and disappeared into what it would appear from a distance might be GUR - Ground Under Repair.

'Damn!' said Ben, 'I just came round too quickly!'

'Don't worry, I'm certain it's Ground Under Repair and you'll be able to drop out.'

'Bad luck old boy,' Marcus cried and proceeded to land his ball on the green twenty five feet from the pin.

'That's more like it. Thanks for the clubbing Seamus.'

'No problem Sir,'

Marcus got to Ben's ball first and said, in a rather triumphant way:

'You've got a tricky bare lie there.'

'That's OK Ben, you can take a free drop not nearer the green,' Tim advised.

'But where's the GUR marker?' asked Seamus mischievously, 'I don't see one anywhere. Sorry. My mistake. It's marked on the grass just over there.'

So rightly, Ben took his free drop and the ball, as luck would have it, rolled back into a small divot.

'What bad luck,' Marcus enthused, 'Still, you've won so many matches here, a little matter of a divot shouldn't cause you too much of a problem, should it?'

So saying he marched onto the green and marked his ball.

Ben studied his shot for a while, and somehow managed to get his club face through the divot and ball, and executed a deft little shot. However it hit a small pitch mark on the green and stopped well short of the hole. He eventually got a six to Marcus's four, and went one down.

Ben was not at all pleased, particularly as Marcus seemed to be gloating. But there were still seventeen more holes and anything could happen. Unfortunately for Ben nothing really happened to cheer him up. His drive at the second landed in the heather, and he scrambled a five to Marcus's par four. Two down. On the third he was bunkered, but played a daring eight iron out onto the green and got his par. But to no avail. Marcus, playing out of his skin, had a birdie three, followed at the next by another, so he stood on the fifth tee, four up. Ben was shattered. His concentration had been rattled at the first and he just couldn't recover. His group was very quiet while Marcus, Siobhan and Seamus were chatting away, and enjoying their undoubted superiority.

'Don't look so down Ben. Surely you've come back from four down before. Clearly you don't want to lose any more holes, particularly a player of your ability, what?'

'Ben listen to me!' said Tim, 'he's getting under your skin. Keep away from him and out of earshot as much as you can. Let me do the talking and rise to his bait for you. Just stay cool, concentrate and swing more freely and slowly. Remember that video I showed you of Ernie Els. That should be your mind-set.' He patted Ben on the shoulder and watched in horror as Marcus's ball pitched on the green to within six feet of the hole.

'Get inside that Ben if you can,' Marcus cried out.

But he didn't, and left himself a tricky twelve foot downhill putt.

'Slightly left to right and it's in,' said Tim encouraging his man.

And in it went, accompanied by much clapping from his friends. Marcus missed, and so Ben was now three down. At the next hole, the sixth, the pond hole, Ben hit the green with a beautifully weighted shot, while Marcus plonked his ball into the water.

Ben made no comment, and went on to win the hole and the next to be only one down at the eighth. Both players parred that one, and the ninth, and then on the tenth Marcus hit his drive left and into the trees. Ben hit the cross bunker, and knew he would take two to get to the green. Meanwhile Marcus, his caddy and Siobhan, were busy looking for his ball, but to no avail. And time was ticking by.

'Why do you keep looking at your watch Tim,' Marcus said irritably.

'Rules are rules, as you said earlier. Since you all went in looking for your ball I've put my watch on you and you've got precisely one minute and forty five seconds left before I deem your ball lost.'

'How dare you!!' Marcus raged 'I've never ever been timed before.'

'Well you are now and it's you who is the stickler for the rules. One minute left,' Tim replied.

The ball wasn't found, and Marcus had to trundle back to the tee and play another, which followed Ben's into the bunker. Marcus had now played three shots, including a penalty for the lost ball, to Ben's one. Ben went on to win the hole, leaving them level standing on the eleventh tee.

But then Marcus smacked his drive at least 280 yards down the fairway.

'Follow that big boy.'

And follow it Ben did, out hitting Marcus by ten yards, but made no comment. Tim's strategy was beginning to pay off as Ben walked off down the fairway on his own, away from the others. And now the match became very tight with the two players halving the next four holes in par, with one birdie each on the fourteenth. It was the sixteenth that nearly caught Ben out. His drive hooked slightly left and when he found it, he was going to have to walk back into some branches to get into a position to play his shot.

As he was positioning himself for the shot, Seamus and Marcus were poring over their Rules of Golf book.

'Our hole I think!' Marcus shouted and Seamus concurred saying,

'Moving or bending a branch while taking a stance is an offence under Rule 13-2. Take a look Tim. It's in black and white.'

But Tim wasn't a dedicated and respected golf professional for nothing. He knew his rules and pointed a little further down the page where it stated quite categorically:

'Except if the player is attempting to take his stance.' But Marcus was not happy, and told Ben to wait so he could see he hadn't broken any branches, which is certainly not allowed in the Rules of Golf. Ben was shocked at Marcus's attitude, and when he was finally allowed to play with no penalty (it would have been loss of hole) he duffed his shot about ten yards into the heather again.

'Bad luck old chap. Sorry to make such a fuss, but rules are rules as we all agreed.'

Marcus's second shot sailed on to the green and he easily won the hole. The match was now coming to a climax with Marcus standing on the seventeenth tee, at one up and two to play.

Marcus was trying to engage Ben in conversation. Ben would have nothing to do with him and went and talked to Clare and Rob.

'Wow! You look drained Rob. I'm the one who should be knackered! Thanks!'

'Do you think you can do it?' They both asked in unison.

'Yup! The seventeenth is my favourite hole and I'm up for a birdie. So don't worry. Like in all good golf stories we'll hopefully finish it on the eighteenth with a win. Keep smiling and keep those fingers crossed.'

Now the seventeenth at West Sussex is a long par four,

with the fairway running downhill left to right, with two bunkers on the right to catch errant drives.

It was Marcus's honour, and he unluckily just caught the top of the second bunker. His ball rolled into the trap.

'Good luck Ben. Don't make my mistake. Always a difficult hole this, particularly for your type of game.'

But Ben was not about to be psyched out, and smashed his drive way over the second bunker, leaving him a simple eight iron into the green.

'Some people have all the luck,' Marcus moaned.

'I think you mean class Mr O'Leary,' Tim retorted.

Marcus duly got out of the bunker, but three putted and finished with a six to Ben's par four. So they now stood level, or all square, with one hole to go.

'Don't forget if we halve the next we carry on until there is a winner,' Marcus bellowed so everyone could hear.

'I don't know about you, darling, but I can't take much more of this pressure. You have to admire Ben's cool attitude,' Rob said said to Clare.

'Since Tim took him aside earlier and gave him a bit of a talking to,' she replied, 'he's seemed much more relaxed and he's not listening to my father's constant chatter which had been getting on his nerves and mine. I'm still confident he can win the match. And if he does we can go in and have lots of champagne to celebrate.'

'Good on you Clare. Let's be positive!'

Both men hit excellent long drives right down the middle, avoiding the bunkers on either side. Ben and Tim were deep in conversation as they arrived at their ball, deciding which club to use.

'I've just got to get this close Tim, and I don't think an eight iron will get me there,' Ben said.

'Trust me. You're so pumped up I'm just afraid that a seven iron will fly the green, and at best, you'll be left on the edge with a monster putt or at worst in the rough at the back.'

Marcus and Seamus's conversation also went along exactly the same lines. In the end both players played from very similar distances, took their eight irons and both landed short of the green, rolling on to it within ten to eleven feet of the pin, with their balls less than five feet apart from each other.

Everyone clapped and hollered. They were both big pressure shots and so it was now down to a single putt to win or halve the match, and go on to extra holes.

Marcus shouted over to Ben, 'No hard feelings I hope. May the best man win.'

Ben ignored this remark and kept walking with Tim towards his ball.

Ben's ball was just the furthest from the hole and as he lined up his putt he didn't think about the £20 million account, or of Clare and Rob's nuptials, but rather of the match itself. He didn't like losing, and he wasn't by nature a loser, and with these thoughts uppermost in his mind he struck the ball firmly. The ball held its line and fell sweetly into the hole.

The noise was deafening and even Siobhan was clapping.

'Quiet now. Give Marcus a chance,' said Ben sportingly.

This was it. Marcus had to hole his putt for the match to continue. He paced up and down with his caddy trying to read the lie of the green and then finally he stood over his ball. He struck it well and it moved from left to right towards the hole at exactly the right speed and everyone waited to hear the inevitable rattle as it dropped into the hole.

'Good putt,' Ben conceded and began thinking about going on to the first extra hole to finish the match. Neither Clare nor Rob dared look and then a strange thing happened. The ball went agonisingly close to the hole and there it sat, teetering on the edge but refusing to go in and then it stopped - stone dead.

Ben was surprised to see Tim walk right up to the hole while looking intently at his watch.

'It's going in,' cried Marcus, 'so now we have to go on to the first to finish the match.' He was kneeling on the ground by the hole willing the ball to drop into the hole. And drop it did, eventually.

'Well played Ben. Your match I believe,' said Tim firmly. 'You Marcus have incurred a one stroke penalty.'

Marcus was apoplectic with rage, 'What?! Don't try your "smart Alec" professionals' tricks with me young man. My ball fell fairly and squarely into the hole. I took three shots and claim the half with Ben and now we go back to the first hole to continue the match,' and he strode off.

'One moment Sir. Please come back,' Tim cried out noticing that Seamus had not followed Marcus but was busily flicking through The Rules of Golf.

'Rule 16-2 entitled, "Ball Overhanging Hole"categorically states that if a player having reached the hole waits more than ten seconds to see if the ball is at rest on the edge of the hole and it subsequently falls in, there is a one stroke penalty.'

'I've never even heard anything so ridiculous in my life. Are you trying to tell me that even though my ball eventually fell in the hole I still receive a penalty stroke just for waiting for the eventuality. I don't believe you.'

'Rules I'm afraid,' said Tim as Seamus, who had eventually found the "said rule", showed it to Marcus.'

'Well it wasn't ten seconds. How can you prove it?'

'I'm afraid I involved your lady wife as I needed a third party to uphold my judgement. As soon as the ball stopped so close to the hole, and you were standing over it willing it in, I told Siobhan I was setting my stopwatch. It happened to me once in a big local tournament and I had to take my opponent's word for it, and like you I wasn't at all happy.'

Then a strange thing happened. Marcus's demeanour changed completely from extreme disappointment to joyful happiness. Smiling hugely he went up to Ben and shook him warmly by the hand, congratulated him on his game and asked him if he'd like his advertising account. He then went over to his daughter, kissed her and shook Rob firmly by the hand and said.

'Congratulations. No hard feelings, I hope you'll both be very happy. And please produce me a golfing grandson or granddaughter. And now, according to the O'Leary Rules of Golf, we repair to the bar. I've already ordered champagne to be chilled and ready, as I felt if you'd lost the match, you'd need it anyway, but now you've won we've all got plenty to celebrate. And the toast will be "business and pleasure", of course!!'

Georgie, and an elated Ben, followed the group towards the clubhouse, hand in hand, fingers entwined, with Ben favouring, as usual, the interlocking grip which had served him so well that memorable afternoon!

MRS ORPWOOD

Life was never easy for Barbara Orpwood. Indeed it would be fair to say that she was Orpwood by name and awkward by nature. Her maiden name had been Rowbotham, so anything was better than that, although strangely she was sublimely unaware of the "awkward" tag. Shortly after marrying Geoff she became pregnant and Darren was born. She only ever wanted one child, as long as it was a boy, so that she could give him her undivided love and attention. This meant Geoff was marginalised and Darren became a spoilt brat.

When Darren was nine years' old, Geoff's work took them to the Midlands. Nobody was sad to see the back of Barbara and Darren, but the general consensus on Geoff was that he was a good man in a tricky marriage, with an over-indulged child. Finding a house had not been as easy as Barbara thought it would be, as she was very, very choosy. Estate agents around Evesham began to dread her phone calls. The houses were either too old, too new, too pricey, too grotty and so it went on. So much so that they still had nowhere to live when it actually came to the move.

'I can't believe that after three months we still haven't found a house. The estate agents round here are pretty useless, don't you think, darling?' Barbara said at breakfast one morning, in the small rented house they had found at the last minute and were using as their base.

Frankly Geoff was glad to start his new job, as Barbara had been particularly awkward since they'd arrived in the Evesham area. According to his wife, who disliked their rented property, the beds were too hard, there was never enough hot water and the shower didn't work. He often remembered that he'd only known Barbara for a few months before he'd married her, and then she'd been all sweetness and light. It was as if a nerve had been activated when the wedding ring was placed on her finger, and Mrs Orpwood felt the need to live up to her name. This she did in Darren's case. He wasn't happy at school, and Barbara had already been round there more than a few times to bully the headmistress and be generally awkward.

'We must be patient. Clearly we have to find the right property but we may need to compromise,' Geoff had insisted.

'Compromise? Compromise? You should know by now that's not a word in my vocabulary. I'm well prepared to take as long as is needed to find the right house. Now off you go and earn some money to pay for all this.'

Fortunately Geoff had an extremely well paid job with an IT company just outside Evesham. He'd set a budget for their new home, but stipulated that it had to be within half an hour's drive from his work.

'Bye darling,' he said kissing her. 'If you find anything likely, fix up a viewing any time after six o'clock this evening. It's light until around nine so I'm very happy to look round as many properties as you want.'

'Okay. I'll take Darren to school then wait for the post, and if necessary go into Evesham. Some of these agents need a good kick up the backside. There seems to be no sense of urgency, and I'm getting very bored with this rented house!'

'Well I'm fed up with school,' moaned Darren, 'I hope we move somewhere with a nice school. Some hope!'

In fact there was one estate agency in Evesham that just about had the measure of Barbara. She was being looked after by a very strong-willed negotiator called Nigel. It was his business, and he'd decided to look after this woman himself. While Barbara could certainly be irascible and difficult, she was also a charmer and instantly took to Nigel, although she wasn't averse to giving him some hard hitting verbals if she felt he wasn't up to scratch.

Nigel put down the phone and took a deep breath. He'd certainly taken a verbal hammering from Barbara.

'Was that Mrs Orpwood?' Sarah, his assistant, asked.

'How did you guess I wonder?' he replied.

'It's just that vacant, resigned look you have after a call from her. I really don't know how you cope. Last week, when you were out for the day, she marched in here as if she owned the place. And when I said there was nothing new on the books she was downright rude. I did tell you didn't I?'

'Yes you did, at least half a dozen times, which doesn't make my job any easier,' Nigel replied.

'Sorry to go on,' said Sarah, 'but she really does get right up my nose and it's so unfair on you.'

'I've spoken to the other agents in Evesham as she's become quite a talking point and, apparently, she's always saying that we're the only outfit really helping her. Is it all worth it, I wonder?' Nigel said resignedly.

Some time later, the door of Flack & Flack was pushed open and in walked the same Barbara Orpwood, bristling with indignation.

'Come now Nigel, clearly I need to come in and see you in person otherwise nothing will be achieved. So what's going on? I've had nothing from you lot for the last couple of days. I need results and I need them now. I've had enough of living in a rented house. You must find me something, preferably empty, so we can move in straightaway.'

'Do sit down Mrs Orpwood,' (she had done so anyway) 'we're well aware of your requirements, but I was under the impression that you were prepared to take as much time as is needed to find the right property.'

'That was yesterday. I don't want to appear awkward Nigel,' she said flashing a delightful smile his way as Nigel thought "what a stunning woman, but what a pain", 'frankly though I've had enough of our present arrangement. You must have something, surely?'

'You awkward, Mrs Orpwood, never!' he replied, tongue very much in cheek, 'and yes, I promise that I'll find you something, very soon.'

'Promises, promises. You're all the same you estate agents.'

'Be reasonable, please. You've already seen at least twenty properties, all within your price range and area, none of which you've remotely liked.'

'Alright, alright. So I'm very choosy, but that's my prerogative. I tell you what I'll do is talk to Geoff this evening about casting the net slightly further afield, and raising our price limit by 20%. How's that?'

'I discussed that with you last weekend, and you said no way.'

'Well I've changed my mind. I'm allowed to aren't I?'

'Yes of course. But this alters things considerably. Leave it with us. You talk to your husband and if he's in agreement why not come back tomorrow, and we'll take it from there.'

'Excellent idea. Wish me luck!' And she got up to leave. 'One last thing, I don't like low ceilings or doorways.' So saying, she flounced out of the office.

'That's a new one to go with all the other dislikes,' said Sarah. 'Shall I start looking through the files?'

'No way. We'll wait until she comes in tomorrow. Let's not waste time today. We do have other clients to look after!'

It was a beautiful summer's day, and Barbara decided to go on a long drive beyond the original area they'd set themselves, to see if there were other villages with houses for sale she liked the look of. This journey took her right down south-west towards Gloucester, up north to Worcester, then east to Stratford- on-Avon, and south-west to Northleach. The countryside was stunning and Barbara soon mellowed, and began to enjoy herself because, with luck, they might soon be living somewhere around this beautiful area. There were pretty villages with quaint names such as Guiting Power, Stanley Pontlarge, Birts Street, Redanarley D'Abitot, Hidcote Boyce and many others. As she drove along Barbara just knew that something had to crop up soon, and as she rounded a bend near the village of Temple Guiting, lo and behold there was a Flack and Flack estate agent's sign and the most divine cottage she'd ever seen. She stopped the car in front of the property's hedge. There was a short drive, but even Barbara felt she shouldn't sweep up it. She got out of the car and took a longer and closer look at the property beyond the gate. It really was a lovely, large, white-washed cottage with roses growing up around the front door, and was perfectly symmetrical, with four windows to the left and four to the right. She absolutely loved it and though to herself,

"This is it. This must be it."

The gate was closed with the name Willow Cottage on it. She hadn't really taken in the garden, but over to the right was a splendid weeping willow, and quite a large pond with a small gazebo overlooking it. Curiosity got the better of Barbara, and she opened the gate with a view to ringing the front doorbell and asking, having checked with the agent, to be shown round. However, after noisily scrunching up the drive she noticed that the garden badly needed weeding and that when she looked through a window, she saw there was no furniture. She clapped her hands in glee.

'Couldn't be better,' she said out loud, as she skirted round the house which was much larger than she'd imagined. At the back there was a sizeable enclosed terrace from which there were views down a lawned garden, all very overgrown, and then onto fields in the distance. She reckoned there was about an acre and a half of garden, which was just perfect. She looked in all the other windows. The kitchen would obviously have to be replaced she thought, and all the rooms looked in need of repair. Certainly decoration was clearly needed throughout, although the ceilings appeared to be high enough.

"What a lovely house. This is definitely the one." And her heart leapt for joy. She didn't really know who to phone first, but decided once she got back in the car to call Nigel at Flack and Flack. And so she did rightaway.

'I've just seen Willow Cottage, Nigel. I love it. I must have it, whatever the price. It's so adorable.'

'Wait a minute. Firstly it's way outside your limit, and secondly it's under offer,' he replied.

'How much is it?' She inquired apprehensively.

'£1.1m.'

'And what's the offer then?'

'£1m, but it needs a lot of work done.'

'Once I've discussed it with Geoff our limit will match it, don't you worry. I'd like to see it at seven o'clock this evening and don't let anyone else see it. Okay?'

'Fine. I'll come out there myself. I live quite near in Snowshill.' As he said that he realised he'd probably made a noose for his own neck.

'That's wonderful. So, if we get it, you'll be able to recommend local builders, plumbers and electricians or whatever, I'm so excited. See you at seven o'clock.'

'Okay. See you then.' Nigel replied, not feeling that happy.

As it was now lunchtime, and after she'd phoned Geoff about the seven o'clock meeting, Barbara took herself off to the local pub in the village.

The landlord told her that the Hawksfields used to live at Willow Cottage, and that the husband, James, had been posted abroad three months ago but was in no great hurry to sell the cottage. The locals all felt it was too highly priced, as it needed a lot of work doing to it. There had been a great deal of interest at first, but people had been put off by the price.

On her way back through Evesham, and after picking up Darren from school, she went by Flack and Flack and picked up the details of Willow Cottage, as she couldn't wait until later that evening. Anyway it would give Geoff and her a chance to study them on their way over.

Back at Flack & Flack, Sarah said to Nigel.

'You've got to try and do a deal for Mrs Orpwood. That way we get her off our backs.'

'You're right, but I shouldn't have let her know I live locally. Big mistake. Having said that, I like Geoff, and if they get the house and once they're settled in Mrs Orpwood may, just may, become less awkward. After all she's an attractive, bright woman, and I'm sure there's some good there, somewhere. Geoff's too nice a guy to have married a complete nightmare!'

'Nigel. Has the offer on Willow Cottage been accepted yet. I don't think it has, has it?'

'I'll check it out before I see them this evening. I know it takes time with Mr Hawksfield working somewhere out in India.'

Meanwhile, after they met back at their rented home Geoff said,

'But darling the price is over £100,000 more than we originally budgeted for; that's if you want the swimming pool put in right away, and what about the new kitchen and all the redecorating you are talking about. And that's just downstairs. I must admit, though, these particulars make it look very appealing. I like the workshop in the garage which I could easily turn into a study and dark room.'

'You wait until you actually see the cottage. The particulars don't do it full justice. How about the location?'

'After you phoned, I looked on the map and of course it is the wrong side of Evesham for the Copthorne Industrial Estate. What I'll do is a dummy run morning and evening later this week, but I don't think it'll be too bad.'

'Oh darling. I'm so happy. I'm absolutely sure we're all going to love it.'

'I hope so, I really do. But you must remember we have to watch our budget,' he said thinking to himself perhaps he could stretch to 25%, as his income had gone up by over

30% since the move.

'Swimming-pool! Swimming-pool! We must have a swimming-pool!' Darren shrieked.

'We will darling, don't you worry,' Barbara replied.

Once they'd arrived at Willow Cottage and met Nigel, Darren spent the whole time rushing around the garden and then from room to room, generally being a nuisance. It soon became apparent that a lot needed to be done, although what it offered with four bedrooms, two bathrooms, a large kitchen, dining room, and a good sized sitting room was exactly what the Orpwoods had specified.

Nigel patiently watched them as they discussed the merits of each room in some detail, but that was his job and it was good to see that they were both obviously enchanted by the cottage. An hour later they repaired to the pub to discuss what action to take next. Just as they were ordering their drinks Nigel's mobile rang.

'It's me Sarah. I just haven't had a chance to call you until now. Parents' meeting for Johnnie, sorry. Anyway, good news for the Orpwoods. Not only has the original offer just fallen through, but Mr Hawksfield's solicitors phoned to say that the owner wants to get on with the sale, and is therefore prepared to accept their offer of £1m. Good luck.'

'Thanks Sarah. Goodbye.'

Nigel turned to the Orpwoods and said.

'Some good news for you,' and repeated his conversation with Sarah.

'That's fantastic!' but Barbara was interrupted by Darren.

'I want another Coke, another Coke, another Coke and crisps and crisps and crisps. Now!'

'Yes darling, of course. Geoff please get our Darren what he wants. Now where were we? I remember – the price.' In hushed tones she whispered to Nigel,

'I'm sure that will not be a problem. Let me work on Geoff. Anyway the main thing is Darren loves it, don't you darling?'

'Yeah it's great Mum, but we've got to have a pool. You promised. You promised! You promised!!' He said, his voice getting higher and noisier.

'Yes my dearest. I did promise. But we'll have to talk to Daddy first.'

'No way. A promise is a promise. And you did promise didn't you?'

'Darren please shut up and make less noise,' Geoff said crossly as he handed his son a Coke and a packet of crisps.

'How dare you talk to Darren like that in front of other people. He's rather over excited, aren't you dear?'

Darren then proceeded to burst into tears, sticking his thumb in his mouth in a petulant manner, and went to sit on his mother's knee. Nigel had seen spoilt kids before but this one was unbelievably ghastly. The sooner he got away the better. By now Geoff was looking well hen-pecked, and Nigel realised this was his cue to leave. He really couldn't take any more from this ghastly woman and her even more obnoxious son.

'I must be going. Think it over, and give me a ring in the morning,' and he shook Geoff's hand and hurried out of the pub.

On their way back to Evesham they discussed the whole enterprise in some detail, working out roughly how much needed to be done to each room. It was clear that quite a lot of work was necessary and the best thing to do was to get a rough estimate.

'I know,' exclaimed Barbara, 'Nigel said he only lives up

the road. Let's ask him to recommend a local builder who can give us an idea of what it is likely to cost. Good idea?'

'What about the pool?' Darren asked in a sulky voice from the back of the car, 'you did promise.'

Even Barbara was getting a bit fed up with her little lamb.

'Do stop going on about the pool. One call to a local swimming-pool centre will get us a quote. So please be quiet now darling.'

And so the chain of events was put into place. Barbara ruined Nigel's day the following morning by phoning and saying they were interested, subject to him recommending his local builder to put together an estimate. His builder, Eric Lamb, was a lovely man, and Nigel really didn't want to wish Mrs Orpwood on him. However, business was business, and so he phoned Eric, warned him about Mrs Orpwood by name and awkward by nature, and asked him to give her a call. He also called Geoff to make sure he was up for it and was surprised by his very positive response.

'Please give me twenty-four hours and I'll make you an offer. I can't thank you enough for recommending your builder. I hope it wasn't too much of an imposition. I know my wife can go on a bit.'

A bit, thought Nigel. A lot might be a better description. He'd also briefed Eric to give a realistic figure for a swimming-pool, as he knew he worked closely with Blue Water Pools, providing and fitting paving stones around new pools. It seemed to Nigel that the pool quote was the key, since that ghastly Darren clearly had to have his way. If that wasn't right it could be no sale for Flack and Flack.

That evening Nigel and his wife, Jane, were sitting quietly having drink on their terrace when Eric came round the corner of the house. He didn't look a happy man.

'Hi Eric, what brings you here and what'll you have?'

'Something very strong,' he said lowering himself wearily into a chair.

'It sounds like this Orpwood lady Nigel was telling me about has lived up to her name,' Jane surmised.

'Do you know something? I've never met such a difficult woman in my life. She's bad enough, but she decided to take her son Darren out of school and he's indescribable. He spent the whole time whingeing and being of no use whatsoever. At one stage I nearly clipped him, he was that cheeky to me. And if I hear anyone saying, "You promised me a pool. You promised me a pool," once more, I'll become a plumber.'

'Here. This whisky should set you up. I'm sorry you've had such a bad time with them, but you did say in the pub the other day that things were a bit quiet.'

'I'd rather be quiet than deal with her. Honest. I'll do the estimate as agreed, and then she can make some other builder's life hell.'

'Frankly. I don't blame you. As a matter of interest how much is a pool these days and what's the normal size.'

Eric explained that the actual standard size was 10m x 5m which she was happy with, but she was keen to have it just four foot six deep all round so that her darling little brat of a boy couldn't drown, and that would be about £25,000. Otherwise a standard six foot deep pool would be about £30,000.

Eric left after his second large one, and went home to prepare his estimate, which he phoned through to Mrs Orpwood the following morning.

'You have to remember Mrs Orpwood,' he said on the phone, 'that this is really only a guesstimate as you may change things as you go along.'

'Thank you so much Mr Lamb. It all seems fine. I'll call you.' But she had no intention of using him. He was so rude to dear Darren and quite off-hand with her.

Barbara took Darren out of school at lunch, and met her husband in their favourite pub near Evesham.

'Well darling. There are all the figures, can we go for it?' she asked.

'While we made a profit selling in Kent, and admittedly houses here are less expensive, the total cost is much more than I planned for. But I do accept we all love Willow Cottage, it would make an ideal home and as you know I've tried the journey in the rush hour, and it really wasn't too bad at all.'

'Don't forget the pool Daddy. You promised,' the ghastly child said.

'Actually it was your mother who promised,' he said, giving her a look, 'as far as I'm concerned it's an unaffordable luxury.'

'But Mum promised. And a promise is a promise,' he said petulantly.

'What I'll do is take this estimate back to my office, talk to my bank and building society and make my decision this evening.'

'Our decision darling, I think,' Barbara said, cunningly putting the boot in.

And so that evening the three of them, (Darren never went to bed until at least ten o'clock), sat down to discuss Willow Cottage. Geoff's calls to his bank and building society had been fruitful, the only sticking point was the extra £25,000 - £30,000 or so that was needed for the swimming pool. His bank manager was adamant that this was not a necessity, and should only be considered once all the building works had been completed. He did point out that they were only working from a loose estimate and that in his experience, costs normally ran over by approximately 20%.

'So there you have it,' Geoff said, 'for the moment it's Willow Cottage, but without the pool.'

Darren was stunned, shouted some obscenity at his father and said, "you promised" to his mother and rushed out of the room in tears.

'I'm sorry Barbara, but it was you who promised. You must sort it out with him. It's quite simple. I just don't have enough money at the moment. We need to wait at least a couple of years before we can consider it. Unless of course you can do without the new kitchen,' he added.

'Don't be so stupid. You know I can't. I know you think I spoil Darren but...'

'You certainly do,' he interrupted.

'Do please be quiet! Let me finish. It may be no bad thing that he has to wait. Even I'm finding him difficult at the moment, and his teachers despair of him. Okay on my head be it. I'll go and talk to him now. But please now, let's get on with Willow Cottage, I'm so excited,' she said bending over Geoff and giving him a kiss.

'Hey, steady darling,' he said laughing.

In the end the purchase did go through, the Orpwoods moved in and the building works commenced straightaway. Geoff kept his head down at the office while Barbara succeeded in upsetting her builder, her plumber, her electrician and her kitchen designer. At one stage all of them decided they'd had enough of her, and insisted on a meeting on site which her husband had to attend. So far there'd been little sign of Geoff, but the workmen only agreed to carry on working for the Orpwoods if Geoff took control, and was on site daily, for at least twenty minutes every morning.

'It's disgraceful,' fumed Barbara after the meeting had finished, 'how can you be expected to know exactly what's going on day to day, when you have a job to do. It's not as though I'm difficult, it's just my eye for detail that upsets them. I think we should fire the lot of them and start again.'

'Is that wise darling, a third of the way through the works?' he replied.

'Yes, if that's the way it's going to be! How on earth, with your office hours, can you be expected to be here every day. You can say what you like, I'm going to fire the lot of them. I will not be ganged up against. And I don't think you've been very supportive either recently. My only comfort is you Darren. At least he understands me, don't you darling?'

'Of course I do Mummy, you know I do. And I also agree with you. All the people who work here are rude to me and tell me to stop behaving like a spoilt brat. The sooner they go the better.'

And go they did, and were replaced time and time again by new teams of builders, and naturally the works escalated out of control - as did the cost.

Geoff despaired. The building works and decoration were nearly completed and Darren, despite being told that the pool would have to wait, expected the pool to be built.

Hardly a day went by without his son reminding him of his mother's promises and he'd also told everyone at school that he would soon be getting a swimming pool.

The miracle was that the local school had put up with him for so long. As you can imagine, he was not a popular child. This was not helped by the fact that some of the children's fathers had worked for the Orpwoods and been fired.

Darren was so thick-skinned it didn't worry him much, but being a frail child and very much mother's pet, he was an obvious target for bullying.

The ringleader of Darren's year was George, who certainly didn't believe his swimming-pool story and made sure this got round the school. Darren was soon branded "a spoilt liar", as well as "awkward Orpwood".

After a while most of the children at his school would chant, "Darren's a spoilt liar, Darren's a spoilt liar" whenever they could. The teachers did little to stop it, as they too had had enough.

Darren didn't like it at all, but decided there was only one way out. He'd invite George over for tea one Saturday (no one from the school had been to his house) and tell his mother to put him in the picture. That should do the trick he thought.

'Of course Darren is going to have a swimming-pool, aren't you my darling?' Darren's mother said the following Saturday over tea.

'See George. What did I tell you? My mother made a promise and she doesn't go back on her word!'

'Now George,' said Barbara. 'The pool will be in next summer at the latest. It's about time all this teasing stopped, don't you agree?'

'S'pose so Mrs Orpwood. Can we come over and swim if Darren stops boasting about it?'

'I don't see why not, do you Darren? We'll have a big party next summer and you can invite your whole form?'

'Wicked Mrs Orpwood. Thanks so much for the tea and see you next summer, if not before,' and George left to cycle home.

You might have expected things to have improved for

Darren at school, but he became even more full of himself now that his form knew the truth, and that they would all be coming to the opening of the swimming-pool.

'Only if you behave yourself and don't tease me,' he would say. 'I can uninvite people you know.' And he would have done although "Fooly pooly" was preferable to "Darren's a spoilt liar".

Summer turned into winter and, the Orpwood's home slowly stopped looking like a building site, so that by Christmas all the work was completed.

Along with the many presents Darren received, was an envelope with a note inside saying,

"I promise the bearer of this note that I will give him a swimming pool within six months."

'Hooray, hooray!' screamed Darren. 'Now I can show this to my class at school and they'll have to believe me.'

Geoff's job had been going extremely well, and he'd been given a hefty bonus, hence the go-ahead for the pool. He dreaded to think what would have happened if there had been no bonus. His wife and son would not have been impressed. Anything for a quiet and easy life, he thought.

But life was not going to be quiet and easy, not if Barbara and Darren had anything to do with the planning of the pool.

To this day Mr Appleton, Blue Water Pools sales manager, still shudders at the thought of Mrs Orpwood, her horrible son and the whole drama of building their pool.

Geoff kept well out of the initial stages, saying once everything was planned and the deposit needed he would then have had his say. He told Mr Appleton he was just paying for it, and that he should deal directly with his wife. That was bad enough, but invariably Darren became involved as well. Mr Appleton's two daughters were at Darren's school, happily not in the same form, so he knew all about the little spoilt brat.

The first sign of trouble came when Barbara and Darren visited the Blue Water Pools facility, which had four different pools on show. They disagreed violently with each other over length, depth, tiles, lining, steps and even the surrounds.

Mr Appleton had to forcibly tear them apart as Darren snapped angrily at his mother.

'Please, please,' said Mr Appleton, 'there are other customers here. Rant and rave in your own home, not here please. The budget I've been given by your husband is, as you well know, Mrs Orpwood, not to exceed £25,000. My suggestion is the Blue Lagoon pool which is ten metres by five. A very decent size pool for your requirements and, yes, I do sort of understand why you want it four foot six deep everywhere.'

'It's just that I know Darren wants all his friends to come round and I don't want the responsibility of anyone drowning and four foot six just seems sensible!'

Unkindly Mr Appleton thought... "friends, what friends?" Still he was getting somewhere.

'But Mum that's so boring. I want to be able to dive in and do bombs without hitting the bottom,' Darren wailed.

'I'm sorry darling but my mind is made up. Do you build many like ours Mr Appleton?'

'What tends to happen is the customer reverts back to the conventional deep and shallow-ended pool. I do see your logic, but your son does have a point. Don't forget he'll soon be over five foot.'

'Sorry, but I disagree. Now will you please follow me

home and we'll choose a site?'

If choosing a pool was difficult, siting it was worse. It took over two hours for Mrs Orpwood and her son to finally agree. Mr Appleton immediately asked if Mr Orpwood was around to bring some order to the proceedings.

'No, he's away on business,' Mrs Orpwood replied tersely, 'now that's all settled can you give me a start date?'

'Well, it looks like sometime in the late spring, during March or April.'

'April would be ideal as we're joining my husband who'll be away on business in South Africa.'

'Fine. I'll put it in for April and phone your husband for the deposit,' said Mr Appleton, getting away as soon as he could. He couldn't believe his good luck that Mrs Orpwood had agreed the building should take place when they were away. He was a happy man, but sadly he'd misread Mrs Orpwood's mood. She phoned him continuously over the next month about minor matters, had him out on site twice because she wanted to re-site the pool, and was not sure that her husband was happy with the four foot six scheme. What this meant was that Mr Appleton could not get an accurate quote together for at least a month. When Mrs Orpwood had finally agreed the total package and the four foot six depth, he visited Mr Orpwood at his office with two quotes, the second one for a six foot deep end with a diving-board and three foot at the shallow end.

Mr Orpwood had always been against the shallower option but, as usual had, in the end, been talked round to it by his wife.

'Tell me Mr Appleton,' he said, offering him a coffee and biscuits, 'if I was to change my mind just before we went away would that be alright.'

'No problem at all. The original deposit on the shallower pool you're about to give me will cover it. Just let me know. A phone call will do it as I'm sure you'll be very busy prior to your trip to South Africa.'

'I'm sure I will, and Mr Appleton I can't thank you enough for all you've done. I know it's not been easy. Believe me I do know,' Geoff said with a twinkle in his eye.

'Not wishing to speak out of turn too much. I'll be glad when it's done and dusted. I think the worst's over, and of course it does help you being away when we're on site.'

'I quite understand. Here's a cheque for the deposit and good luck.'

'Thank you Mr Orpwood,' Mr Appleton said shaking him firmly by the hand, 'I wish you'd been more involved all along.'

'That's my wife and son for you,' Geoff said laughing.

Both the Orpwoods and Mr Appleton assumed, unless there was a late change of mind, that everything was sorted, and Blue Water Pools would be building a four and a half foot deep pool. But they'd ignored the Darren factor. Darren was not happy. He wanted a proper grown up pool, and for once his Dad after much discussion with his son agreed, at the expense of his wife's more than likely wrath.

'I am not having another word said about the matter. You, Geoff, have taken no interest in the pool whatsoever, and frankly Darren you're very lucky we're having one at all,' she fumed one evening after supper.

'The point is Mum it's two against one,' Darren said in a whingeing voice.

'No Darren, the point is it's now all done and dusted and I will not discuss the matter any more. The subject is closed.'

Not so for Dad and son. Darren decided that as it was his

Dad who was paying, he should have the final say.

The Saturday morning before Geoff went to South Africa and when Barbara was out doing some last minute shopping, Geoff and Darren had a long chat about the pool and eventually agreed that his Dad should ring Blue Water Pools and order the other six foot deep pool with a five foot high diving-board.

'It could be divorce you know Darren,' his Dad said ruffling his son's hair.

'No way, I'm sure once we get back, and she sees it and swims in it she'll love it. Can you tell them to have the heating cranked up for when we get home? I want to swim in it right away. You're cool Dad.' And for probably the first time in their lives they actually saw eye to eye.

Geoff didn't feel that cool about double-crossing his wife, but in some ways he'd rather have Darren as an ally than Barbara. As Darren had said - "she would soon get used to it".

Later that morning, Geoff phoned Mr Appleton to tell him the news.

'I think that's a good decision, but what does your wife feel about it?' he asked.

'Don't bother about her, that's my problem. And don't forget the five foot diving-board.'

'That's fine. We'll have to construct that first before we build the pool.'

'Okay, fine. I'm off on Wednesday so I hope it all goes well. My wife and Darren will be following me shortly. If we think of any thing else we'll be in touch. Cheers. By the way do you need it in writing?'

'No, this call's fine,' he said and rang off.

Mr Appleton was well pleased with their decision. He

was sure it would give them far more enjoyment and as an added bonus, it was going to cost a bit lot more than Mrs Orpwood's original order. Thank God they were going to be away, and he could get on with it in peace.

The build started the following week, with the first job being to construct the diving-board. Then the excavation would commence.

Imagine Mr Appleton's horror, but no great surprise, when, a few days later, he received a fax, of all things, from Mrs Orpwood, somewhere on safari in South Africa. It read:-

Just to confirm our pool is four foot six deep as per our contract and will be ready and heated on our return, April 30th.

It had been sent on plain paper with no fax reference or address which was clearly what Mrs Orpwood wanted. So there was no way he could contact her as the situation was out of his control.. He didn't even have Geoff's mobile number nor could he remember his office's name or location. He knew who wore the trousers and he knew whose instructions he should follow, particularly as these were the last he'd received with the contract. Also he'd only verbally agreed the larger pool with Mr Orpwood so there was no back-up paperwork. The diving board was up, but taking it down would have to wait as most of the excavation was now completed and would have to be filled in to a depth of four foot six. And it would have to be done quickly to get the job done on time for their return. What a bugger! Mr Appleton thought and added "What a bitch!'"

As it happened the Orpwoods arrived home just after Mr Appleton's team had left after putting the finishing touches to the pool. It was a bright and sunny day, perfect for a dip, and as you can imagine, dear reader, Darren was in a state of high excitement. As they pulled up outside their front door, he got out of the car and rushed round the side of the house, stripping off as he ran across the garden towards the pool, until he was just in his swimmers.

He quickly climbed up to the top of the 5 ft diving-board and stood there shouting,

'Mum and Dad, this is soooooooo cool! You must come and watch me dive in, now!'

Meanwhile, his father had just picked up a weird message on the answerphone, saying Blue Water Pools would be round the following day to take something away. He couldn't hear the rest of it, so he went out into the garden to see Darren standing on the top of the diving board with the water far below him, glistening invitingly.

'Dad. Mum. It's wicked. Watch me!' Just before he launched himself into the pool Geoff heard his wife screaming hysterically and running frantically down the garden towards the pool.

'No! Stop! Now! Oh my God!' as Darren's head hit the water and a milli-second later his head cracked open on the bottom of the four foot six swimming pool.

The one that Mrs Orpwood had always wanted.......

HAVOC

Dave knew the woods at the back of his house better than anyone else in Lower Edgeworth. This was not only because he was born and brought up there, but also because he was now the head gamekeeper for Lord Edgeworth's shoot. He had a tied cottage in the village where he and his wife lived.

One of his children, Joanna, was living in nearby Upper Edgeworth with her boyfriend Mark, whilst his other daughter, Emily, was just finishing university. They were a very happy and popular family and keen churchgoers, Dave being a church warden and his wife, Betty, doing the flowers most Sundays.

So, there you have it. A family that did no wrong and lived in quiet harmony, one for the other, and well liked locally. That was until that eventful Sunday in early November.

On that fateful day, Dave was out in the woods with his springer spaniel, aptly named Havoc, checking on the pheasants, and spoiling them by putting down grain in the deeper covers. Suddenly, Havoc stood as still as a statue. When Dave caught up with her, he could see why. There in the distance were two men having what looked more than just an argument. Dave could not really distinguish what was being said, but there were certainly a lot of heated expletives. He was unsure, but thought that perhaps he recognised one of them as a regular in his local pub. Dave quietly put a lead on Havoc and started walking towards the men, to see if he could help out in some way. Suddenly he heard a shot and the man he didn't recognise fell forward to the ground.

'Oh my God!' Dave exclaimed, forgetting how near he was. The other man got up and turned round abruptly.

'Who's there?' he said, running through the undergrowth, shooting wildly in Dave's direction. Dave felt a searing pain in his shoulder. He had been hit and he slumped to the ground, letting go of Havoc, who wisely scampered off. Dave lay there, inert, and barely breathing.

'You stupid bastard,' the gunman said, kicking Dave's head viciously several times.

'For your sake I hope you saw nothing.' And he turned away in disgust and ran off through the woods. Dave knew nothing of this though. He just lay there in a semi-conscious state, bleeding heavily.

Havoc's sixth sense told her that her master was in trouble, and that meant getting home as quickly as possible.

Betty had just returned from the village shop when she saw Havoc running towards her across the garden. Instinctively she knew something was wrong as there was no sign of Dave, and Havoc's lead was trailing behind her. The dog came panting over to her, jumped up as Betty took off her lead and then ran off back the way she had come from, with Betty following as quickly she could.

'I hope this isn't some new game you and Dave have devised.' But she didn't think it was.

Betty had often walked along the outside of Coombe Wood, but had never too keen to actually enter too far into it. The woods were spread over three square miles and were very dense near the centre, which is where it appeared Havoc was taking her. Dave had probably fallen and twisted his ankle, she thought. Silly man!

When she found him at last, she was horrified by what she saw. There was blood everywhere, and he appeared to be dead.

'Oh my God! Dave what's happened to you?' and as she knelt down she noticed he was still breathing, but only just. Betty was a competent woman, and immediately took out her mobile and phoned Dr Reid at his surgery in the village. She was very relieved when he eventually answered his phone.

'You think he has been shot? he said. 'I don't believe it, in Edgeworth? Why? Sorry Betty enough of my prattle. Keep him warm and see if you can staunch the blood. It sounds, by your description, as though he's been shot in the shoulder. If, as you say, you're in Coombe Wood directly behind your house, Sabre will be able to pick up Havoc's most recent scent. I'll come right away. My patients will have to wait . I'm also going to call an ambulance and have it on stand-by at your house.'

Sabre, his black labrador, could not believe her luck, as Dr Reid's wife had just taken her for a walk and they had only been back ten minutes or so. She had no trouble picking up Havoc's scent, and Dr Reid was with Betty within a few minutes.

'Thank God you're here, Richard. I'm so worried. Will he be alright? He looks so white and haggard.'

'That's probably shock. I'll give him a jab to ease the pain and then you and I will stay with him until the para medics arrive.'

Just then Dave opened his eyes, and, with difficulty he kept on repeating six words "I think I've seen a murder" time and time again until he lapsed back into semi-consciousness .

'How bizarre,' Dr Reid said, 'maybe he did and that's why he was shot. Once he's on the mend we'll get the whole story, but for now let me turn him into the correct position to help staunch the blood. There. Is that the dogs barking over there? I wonder why. I'll go over and have a quick look. Please stay here Betty.'

Having found out why the dogs were barking Dr Reid came back to Betty saying.

'The man over there has been shot in the throat, and he's dead I'm afraid. What a horrendous thing to happen. Let's hope Dave can shed some light on what occurred. It would appear he may have witnessed something dreadful and has, sadly, paid the price. I'll quickly inform the police of what's taken place.'

After he'd made the call on his mobile, they waited patiently for the paramedics and the police to arrive. The wonders of modern science had taken them directly to the scene.

'I suggest you go with the ambulance Betty and I'll sort the police out. Ah! Here they are now. Good afternoon. I'm Dr Reid, and this is Betty Parsons, this poor unfortunate fellow's wife. Her husband did briefly regain consciousness and said over and over again - "I think I've seen a murder. I think I've seen a murder." He is clearly in a state of shock, and I would advise you Constable that you leave off talking to him until tomorrow, by which time he should have stabilised, and then you can take a statement.'

'That's fine Dr Reid, and now can you take us to the scene

of the crime please.'

'By all means. This way, follow me.'

By early evening Coombe Forest was heaving with policemen, forensics and a multitude of other interested parties. Betty had stayed at the hospital for a quite a while, as Dave had deteriorated and was now unconscious. By the time she left, exhausted by the afternoon's events, she had contacted both her daughters, who were now at home comforting her. Dr Reid popped in about 9 o'clock that evening to say that the police had not been able to identify the body, and that they were doing house to house interviews to see if anyone in the village had any useful information.

Unusually for such a small village, it had a police station. This was now being used as The Ops Room, and the village policeman, PC Paul Livermore, was feeling very important, particularly as CID had asked him to nominate any villagers who might have been involved.

'There's only really one bad apple here in Lower Edgeworth.'PC Livermore said. It's really a family affair, the Frasers, as old Albert Fraser was court-martialled in the last war, then his son Gerry's building business got done by the VAT man and his other son, Sean, has never been able to hold down a job for more than a few months. Last time I heard anything about him he was apparently peddling drugs in Plymouth. Neither the Plymouth police nor I have been able to pin anything on him. His alibis are always rock solid, in a family kind of way, if you get my meaning!'

'Right then. We'll start with the Frasers and then visit the other houses in the village,' said Detective Inspector Lawson. 'It may be that someone saw him around the woods this afternoon.'

'Very unlikely, sir. The villagers are all frightened of the Frasers. No one here would ever dare grass on them. I have to say though that Sean seems an unlikely suspect, as I've never known him as that violent.'

'Well, we'll see him any way. I suggest you stay here and help man the Ops Room. You said it's Downland Cottage just past the pub?'

'That's right. You can't miss it. Good luck and see you tomorrow,' Paul shouted as they left the station. 'You'll need it.'

And he was proved right. Everyone in the village had water tight-alibis, no one more so than the Frasers.

Early the following morning Betty received a phone call from the hospital with the good news that Dave had regained consciousness, eaten a hearty breakfast and his wound was healing very satisfactorily. However, what they couldn't understand was that he would not converse with anyone, or even try to write anything down. He appeared to have total amnesia.

'Very strange,' said Betty. 'I'll come right over.'

When she arrived she was taken aside by the specialist who had been treating Dave.

'I'm sorry about this but your husband seems to have lost the will to speak and write. There are marks on his skull where it looks as though he has been kicked very hard quite a few times. This may explain his loss of speech, which is very possibly linked to amnesia. However, total non- communication is very rare. See how he reacts to you. He may be more positive.'

Betty sat with Dave all day, talking to him softly whilst holding his hand and trying to get some sort of response. She gave him pen and paper. But nothing. He just stared into the distance, only smiling when she told him about Havoc coming to find her. That was about the only reaction she could get. Although she visited him two or three times a day, and he physically grew stronger and stronger, nothing in his brain seemed to click. He was discharged after a few days and subsequently visited at home by an eminent local psychiatrist, Dr Hume, who confessed that he had never come across a case like this.

'Normally,' he told Betty, her daughters and PC Livermore in the Parsons' kitchen one morning later that first week, 'there is some sort of recognition to questions, or at the very least, something in writing. You say the only time he smiles is when you talk about Havoc saving the day. At least that's something. He does have some cognitive awareness, although of course he doesn't appear to recognise anyone or anything else at all. I'm afraid I'm at a loss as to what to recommend. It is very likely that once he is back at work, out with his pheasants and running the shoot, things will come back to him. So, for the moment, lots of rest and TLC from you all. You have been wonderful as a family, but now I think you girls should get back to your own lives, and let Dave sort himself out as best he can.'

Meanwhile, the hunt for the killer gathered momentum. Sean, it would appear, had been none too clever. A couple of days after the murder, at a further routine interview with him, one of the CID detectives asked if he could take a closer look at his boots, which he'd remembered had been caked in mud.

'Do what you like. As long as I have them back for tomorrow. But don't go pinning anything on me, I often walk in Coombe Forest.'

'So you won't mind if I take a look at those gloves as well,' said the detective pointing at some gloves lying by Sean at the table. Sean coloured slightly but was ostensibly glad to oblige.

'Go ahead. I often use them when I am out shooting vermin.'

'Do you have a licence?' the detective enquired.

'Of course I do, and my shotgun is kept locked up in my garage in accordance with the regulations.'

'Good. I'd like to take it as well,' he said getting up, putting the gloves carefully in a plastic bag and asking his assistant to pick up the boots.

'Suit yourselves. Remember what I told you, I was at home all that Sunday afternoon helping my father with some paperwork.'

'Fine. Just let me have the shotgun and thanks for your co-operation.'

It did not take forensics long to discover that the cordite on the gloves was not consistent with Sean's shotgun discharge. It had to be from another weapon. Furthermore, not only did the pattern on Sean's boots match those prints found where the original body lay and the trail to Dave's body, but the adjacent undergrowth had been broken by Sean's boots, and small pieces had correspondingly lodged in the sole and laces.

Sean Fraser was brought in for further questioning later that week, when it was discovered that his victim was a former work colleague who had also been dabbling in drugs. He was therefore formally charged with the murder of John Sewell, and premeditated assault causing grievous bodily harm to Dave Parsons. However, the evidence against him was pretty circumstantial, particularly as the murder weapon had not been found. The trial was set for December

15th in Cirencester Crown Court.

Whilst the CID had moved fast, Dave's recovery, if at all, was painstakingly slow. He was back at work and seemingly happy to be up and about. But there was still no recovery of speech or any inclination to write things down, or indeed any recognition of anything at all except his dog and his pheasants. He had even been taken back to the scene of the crime, but showed no emotion at all. His life appeared to be one long trance, and he did not seem to be getting any better. His wife had been warned by the CID that Dave would probably be asked to stand as a witness at Sean's trial, as both Dr Reid and Betty had heard him say "I think I've seen a murder" at least half a dozen times. And that was the last time anyone had heard him utter anything at all.

The prosecuting council, James Shepherd QC, came and visited the Parsons a few days before the trial was due to begin. He was a very articulate and caring man, and explained to Dr Reid, Dave and Betty what would be needed of them in court.

'I will be opening the trial itself with the case for the prosecution, therefore you Betty and Dr Reid will be questioned by me first on how you originally found Dave. Crucially, you will both need to repeat exactly what he said - "I think I've seen a murder". The barrister for the defence will then cross-examine you, but I see no problem there, as both your statements to me will have been straightforward. As far as Dave is concerned, I believe his problem will only be solved by some sort of shock. Clearly I am well aware of Dave's condition, but Dr Hume and I are convinced that Sean's presence in the courtroom could unlock his brain with the impact of seeing him again for the first time since the murder. I will ask the judge to remove Sean from the court just before Dave is brought in and steps into the witness-box. Then Dave will be allowed some time to get used to his surroundings. It will be difficult and confusing for him, but I will obviously stand by him giving him my total support. You must trust my judgement on this. Hopefully, I can somehow release Dave from this awful nightmare, bring back to you the man you love and cherish and nail Sean, all at the same time.'

'I do hope so. And, yes of course you must do what you think is best. But please be gentle with him. Look at him now, he just seems to gaze into thin air. He is like an automaton, religiously going through the motions - getting up, eating, working etc. - although strangely he does seem to have some sort of relationship with Havoc. It is all so sad. So sad,' Betty said quietly wiping the tears from her eyes, 'I'm sorry but it is all too much to bear sometimes. Ask anyone in the village and they will tell you Dave has always been the life and soul of any party, and a kinder person you could not wish to meet. It just all seems so unfair.'

'There, there, Betty. I will see you in court next Thursday, and I think it would be a good idea if both your daughters came. Dave needs all the support he can get. Also I don't think it would be a bad idea if Dave brought Havoc along, almost as his guide-dog. That dog seems to offer some hope for Dave and I think that could, maybe, help on the day. Thank you for the tea. Goodbye Dr Reid, Betty, Dave and you too of course, Havoc. Let's see what we can accomplish together,' James said, stroking Havoc and then letting himself out of the back door.

The trial started in a blaze of publicity, as the case had caught the imagination of the local community. The villagers of Lower Edgeworth had got together and hired a coach to attend the proceedings. They all accompanied the Parsons family to court, as much out of curiosity as in support.

Because it was common knowledge that Dave had uttered those damning six words - "I think I've seen a murder", it was agreed that the case for the prosecution would lead off with Betty Parsons, followed by Dr Reid and finally, for that part of the trial, Dave Parsons. The defence had not been happy about it, but James Shepherd had convinced the judge that the proceedings could be shortened greatly with his proposal.

Poor Betty, although clearly very nervous, and Dr Reid conducted themselves well whilst being questioned by James Shepherd. The barrister for the defence, Russell Daly, was a different kettle of fish, as he had a reputation for being a difficult but intelligent cross-examiner.

'Mrs Parsons. Please refresh my memory. This supposed statement by your semi-conscious husband, "I think I've seen a murder" - was said how many times?'

'At least half a dozen.'

'At least half a dozen. Are you sure? Apparently you made this statement to the police after it was discovered your husband had severe memory loss. Quite convenient really wasn't it? I put it to you that you and Dr Reid dreamt up those words, " I think I've seen a murder". So I'm sorry Mrs Parsons, it just doesn't wash. Clearly these words are not a basis of proof or solid evidence.'

'I object M'Lud,' said James Shepherd jumping to his feet.

'Objection overruled.'

'Next witness please,' said the defence council.

Dr Reid was put through the same grilling as Betty. He became particularly cross when the barrister for the defence said:

'As a respected member of the community you must have felt in your joint statement with Mrs Parsons, that Mr Parsons saying-" I think I've seen a murder", would carry some weight. I disagree. Again, I put it to you that no such thing happened. It seems very clear that Mr Parsons is not going to bring much to these proceedings in his condition.'

Roars of laughter came from Sean's family and friends. 'Order! Order please,' cried the judge. 'Dr Hume to the witness-box please.'

James Shepherd went through his credentials and, questioned him thoroughly on cases of amnesia similar to Dave Parsons' current predicament.

'Only one question, Dr Hume,' said Mr Daly getting to his feet. 'While I am very impressed by your prognosis of Mr Parsons' case, in the circumstances is it fair to assume that he could have uttered just those six words, when clearly he must have been lapsing in and out of consciousness? Wouldn't he more likely have said something to allay his wife's fears. In other words, try to comfort her in some way?'

'No, absolutely not. Remember he had just seen someone shot, and presumably killed. He was then shot himself, by someone running towards him. Think of the shock he must have endured, particularly if it were someone he knew.'

'Fine. But why, when he regained some form of consciousness, didn't he give his murderer a name? It might have saved us all some time and effort.'

Again more mirth from Sean's friends.

'Order! Order!' shouted the judge. 'Please strike out that last sentence. And you, Mr Daly, think yourself lucky not to be censured for your appalling bad taste. Carry on.'

'To answer your question, Mr Daly, simply put, the phrase - " I think I've seen a murder" - means that first and foremost that is what Mr Parsons' brain took on board. He probably would have put a name to it if he had not been shot so soon after witnessing a crime. As I'm sure you know, there are precedents of this type of behaviour after a massive shock. In this case, it would appear that the only fact Mr Parsons had time to take on board was that he was sure he had seen a murder. If he had time between witnessing what he thought was a murder, and being shot, he might well have described the supposed murderer or indeed have known him and been able to use his name. This is irrefutable, as there are cases on record similar to this where more has been taken on board by the protagonist, such as the description of a murderer, or even sometimes his name. In this case it was just one thought process, sadly.'

'The problem is, we have both Mrs Parsons' and Dr Reid's statements of what he apparently said, but we can't exactly cross-examine Mr Parsons can we?' he stated with an obvious snigger.

Mr Shepherd got to his feet and said to the judge, defence and jurors:

'I'm afraid you couldn't be more wrong, as that is exactly what I propose to do.'

There was a general murmur round the court and some cries of 'Shame on you!'

'But this is most irregular M'Lud' shouted Mr Daly jumping angrily to his feet.

'Not so Mr Daly,' the judge interrupted. 'We did agree this prior to the trial, and you had no problem with it then. Perhaps the proceedings so far have not been to your liking, in view of what is now proposed. I'm afraid you will have to sit down, and allow Mr Shepherd to deal with his witness in whichever way he deems appropriate.'

'So be it, your Honour' said Mr Daly, in a resigned manner. At that moment Sean, as agreed, was ushered from the courtroom.

By now Mr Parsons and Havoc had entered the witness box. Dave looked pale and nervous, constantly twiddling his thumbs and scanning the courtroom blankly for over a couple of minutes.

You could hear a pin drop as Sean was ushered back into the courtroom

'M'Lud please could Mr Fraser now be placed ten feet in front of Mr Parsons,' Mr Shepherd asked.

'I object, M'Lud,' shouted Mr Daly.

'Objection overruled. Please continue.'

As Mr Fraser walked forward towards the witness box, Dave Parsons stared at the advancing man, not noticeably taking anything in at all. Mr Shepherd was not at all relaxed, realising that his gamble might well fail, particularly as Sean Fraser was looking anywhere rather than at Dave Parsons.

By now Mr Shepherd was on his feet.

'Please Mr Fraser look at the man in the witness box.'

'Why should I?'

'Because you are in court being tried for murder and you are under oath. Please do as I say.'

'I object, your honour,' Mr Daly countered.

'Objection over....' The judge was not able to finish his sentence as Mr Parsons' eyes locked on Mr Fraser's and he tried to leave the witness box as if he had some unfinished business to settle. By doing so he became caught up in Havoc's lead and fell out of the witness box, banging his head heavily on the stone floor. The courtroom was hushed as he lay there, apparently lifeless.

'Please, please! Leave him,' said his lawyer, realising

what might happen next as the clerks ran across to help.

'I mean it,' shouted Mr Shepherd 'PLEASE leave him.'

'This is most irregular Mr Shepherd,' the judge said.'I'll give you a couple of minutes, and then he must go back into the witness box.'

It seemed a lifetime before Dave Parsons got up, untangled Havoc's lead and walked quietly back to the witness box, where he stood erect. He seemed a completely different man. His faraway look had gone, replaced by one of self-belief, as he gazed knowingly round the courtroom.

'In your own time Mr Parsons,' said the judge.

Before he spoke there was a quiet apprehensive buzz throughout the courtroom.

'Your Honour and members of the jury, I can recently only remember saying time and time again "I think I've seen a murder", but now I'm absolutely positive I did see a murder.'

Following this unlikely turn of events, there was a general murmur of amazement around the court that Mr Parsons had apparently recovered his power of speech. And there was more to come.

'I definitely know that this man, Sean Fraser, standing over there, straight in front of me, shot a poor fellow that afternoon, before he ran towards me, shot me in the shoulder and then proceeded to put the boot in. I then apparently seemed to have lost my nemory completely and I'm sorry but I haven't a clue what happened after that fateful afternoon right up until now. All I know is that I've got a very sore head and a wonderful dog. Thanks Havoc for giving me back my memory and with it, my life.'

And then the courtroom erupted to cries of.

"Guilty! Guilty!" with the judge shouting "Order! Order!"

And while all this was going on, Havoc stood quietly by the witness box, happily wagging her tail.

A Corsican Affair
READ THE FIRST FEW PAGES OF THIS EXCITING NOVEL
FEATURING ROMANCE, KIDNAPPING AND THE SHADY
TRANSACTIONS OF THE CORSICAN UNDERWORLD.
PUBLICATION DATE APRIL 2018.
Thomas Jackson

CHAPTER ONE

LONDON
NUITS ST GEORGES

It was the rain, rain, rain, and still more rain that finally made up my mind. After the wettest May on record, with June and July not doing much better, I decided that I needed a break and a glimpse of blue skies and feel the warmth of the sun again. I'm George, by the way, in my late twenties, a bachelor, blond and tall with dark green eyes. I like to live my life to the full and rely on humour and patience to get me by. Real friendships are important to me and I always relish a challenge, whatever its nature. It keeps me on my toes and adds a bit of spice to one's life. Enough of me.

Before I booked my trip I needed to visit my sister Cara, who had been in a drug re-hab centre for the last couple of months and relied on me for support. Her progress to date had been steady, but I wanted to see her before I left to make sure all was well. In fact when I last visited her she was in a very positive frame of mind. She was determined to kick the habit once and for all, but was still very upset that she'd caused so much distress within our family. I told her she mustn't be , just get better and that we'd always be there to support her. I had always felt that I should have done more to help her. But she was in good hands and she was really pleased that I was going to take some time off, which was exactly what I needed, for at least a week or two.

So I decided to return to Corsica, the fourth largest island in the Mediterranean after Sicily, Sardinia and Cyprus. An island that hankered after independence from France. Corsica was called *Kalliste,* "the most beautiful",, by the Greeks and is still known as

Ile de la Beauté, "Isle of Beauty". There had been some trouble on the island over the last few years, but generally speaking things had apparently quietened down. Corsicans, in general, are proud people who despite the influence of tourism, have maintained their unique character and continue to adhere to century old traditions, often inland away from the coastal resorts.

Last time I was there was in the spring a couple of years ago, when the heavy scent of the Corsican vegetation known as *macchia*, or *maquis*, the wild flowering undergrowth that exists nowhere on mainland France, made it an unforgettable experience. This growth covers nearly one third of the island and is why Corsica is famous for its distinctive and intense "perfumed" aroma, which cannot be found anywhere else in the world. I'd flown direct to Ajaccio, hired a car and done some business combined with pleasure. I'd found the Corsicans a friendly and proud set of people and, although my French is laughably inadequate, I was always made to feel very much at home.

This time, I felt like taking my time and driving through France and over by ferry to Porto Vecchio. The question was, would my old Triumph Vitesse convertible, called Doris, make it? Why on earth not? We'd managed the South of France once before, albeit a few years ago. So I had her serviced, which she passed with flying colours, booked the Channel Tunnel to Calais, the ferry to Corsica and arranged for Debbie, my long-suffering and ex-girlfriend, to look after the business while I was away.

Running a small but thriving antiques shop in Fulham, specialising in porcelain plates and rare pieces of glassware involved me in a number of buying trips, mainly around Britain. However, I had a good excuse for choosing Corsica, as on my previous trips there I'd been very successful in selling some of my porcelain, but more so actually buying unusual French examples, which I then sold on back in London at a good profit. Corsica had proved to be a good place for me to hunt for hidden old Sèvres or Limoges porcelain.

Indeed, when I was last there a couple of years ago, I'd met up with a wonderful dealer with the unlikely name of Carcarille - Monsieur Carcarille to me. I'd bumped into him at an antiques fair in Ajaccio and, because we shared the same interests in porcelain and *le gastronome avec les vins*, we both got on extremely well. Fortunately he spoke very good English, and was always insisting I go and stay with him and his wife in their home in the centre of the island, high up in the hills in a village called Ste Lucie de Tallano, near Sartène. As I'd taken him out for an excellent dinner at Langans on his last trip to London, which had cost me a fortune, I phoned and arranged to stay with him and his wife. He suggested that I should bring some English porcelain with me and he'd try and set up some deals. Now I could certainly justify the trip as business!

So, on a typically cold and damp morning in early July during Wimbledon, Doris, sounding silky smooth and looking immaculate, and I set off for the Channel Tunnel. I didn't really have a care in the world. I was running a fairly successful business, was in rude health and not encumbered with the vagaries of some heavy relationship. So I turned up the rather ancient radio and sped along the M25. Not for long. My euphoria was rudely interrupted. What I hadn't reckoned on was the plethora of orange and white cones that cluttered up the M20, purposefully put out to coincide with the beginning of the holiday season to make sure holiday-makers got off to a stress free start. Some hope!

However after a fast and easy Eurotunnel journey I was soon in France and heading south down the A26 towards Burgundy. I love France. The country has so much to offer. The beautiful language for a start, with its wonderful seductive intonations. So while I'm able to speak a *soupçon* I've always found *ça va* and *bonne journée* encourages *bonhommie,* which often gives the unexpected impression that one can actually speak French. I do believe that the French love it if you make the effort to speak their language however badly, except Parisians!

What I was looking forward to was indulging myself in their food, wine and my favourite aperitif, pastis. So as I motored along as fast as Doris would take me, I marvelled at the lack of traffic. Never the hint of a contraflow. Late that evening I found myself near Nuits St Georges, with nowhere booked, typical me, with only an old Michelin Guide listing the Auberge du Lac as one of their recommendations.

Eventually I found the hotel at the end of a long drive. It had a look of faded elegance but was a very welcome sight after my long journey. After parking Doris, Itook out my suitcase and wandered in.

The cool, green eyes of the girl behind the reception desk looked up from the magazine she was idly perusing and said.

'Bon soir Monsieur.'

'Bon soir. Est-ce que possible avoir une chambre pour la nuit?'

As I said this, I became painfully aware of my lack of French which was a shame as this lady was more than just beautiful, more drop dead gorgeous. Knowing my luck she was probably married with children or going out with the chef.

However, she smiled a smile that made my heart miss a few beats.

'Certainly monsieur, you can have our last available room and also dinner is still being served. So perhaps it's your lucky night?' she said in a very provocative way.

'A CORSICAN AFFAIR' WILL BE PUBLISHED IN APRIL 2018.

....